In the world of Deathlands

There were, of course, survivors...

The world was not destroyed—just a way of life. The global population was cut down to perhaps one-fifth of what it had been. The ecosystems were utterly disrupted. The climate was transformed.

In what had once been North America, the survivors struggled to prevail in a new age of plague, radiation sickness, barbarism and madness. There were days of seemingly endless night, eerily lit by fires in the sky. Pyrotoxin smogs blanketed the earth. Fetid strontium swamps created new and terrible life forms. Two-hundred-mile-an-hour winds hurtled across the landscape, and when by some freak chance a storm cloud swept in from the sea, it was acid rain that fell— pure acid that stripped a man to the bones in sixty seconds of shrieking agony.

In spite of this, life returned.

In isolated pockets, survivors fought back against terrible odds. And won.

Sort of.

JAMES AXLER

DEATH LANDS

Red Holocaust

A GOLD EAGLE BOOK FROM

W❂RLDWIDE

TORONTO · NEW YORK · LONDON · PARIS
AMSTERDAM · STOCKHOLM · HAMBURG
ATHENS · MILAN · TOKYO · SYDNEY

This is for MH who made me believe
in the reality of the *deus ex machina*.
With thanks and the best of friendship.

First edition September 1986

ISBN 0-373-62502-2

Printed in Canada

Chapter One

RYAN CAWDOR BLINKED, wincing as he tried to sit up. The lights still glowed in the patterned metal plates set in the floor and ceiling. The armored glass walls were pale blue streaked with gray. Instinctively his hand fell to the smooth butt of the SIG-Sauer P-226 9 mm pistol on his hip.

There was the now-familiar feeling of nausea as he backed against the wall, shaking his head to clear the cobwebs of the mat-trans jump. Only a frozen moment ago he and his colleagues had been facing death in the Darks, the mountainous region that had once been called Montana. Now they were . . . ?

"Where the firestorm are we?" he muttered.

It was their fifth jump within an hour. Each one had been accompanied by a gut-wrenching sickness and a whirling in the brain, as if every single particle of tissue was being dissolved and spun through a suction pump.

Ryan couldn't even begin to think how the complex machines might work. Probably nobody now alive had any ideas. All of that came from before the war.

NEARLY A HUNDRED YEARS had passed since Doomsday—high noon on the twentieth day of January in the year of our Lord 2001. The last day of our Lord. The missiles rose and the skies darkened. The death toll was countless and humanity stood on the brink of extinction. But there were survivors. There will always be survivors.

From the caves and mines and shelters, they emerged to find a changed world where a nuclear winter raged for nearly a generation. But again there were survivors. And they bred and their children bred.

Three generations and close to a hundred years passed. Most of the United States was changed. Deserts in Texas, Arizona and New Mexico became fiery nuke hot spots where storms carrying rain of undiluted acid howled in from the Gulf. Most of California had slipped unprotesting into the seething Pacific. Volcanoes and earthquakes had changed the maps forever.

Except that there weren't any maps.

On the East Coast, the big cities crumbled in the endless rain. From the lawless elements rose a new breed of leader, barons who ran their own fiefdoms like medieval lords, paying armies of mercenaries to protect and expand their borders.

In the middle of the country, known as the Death-lands, civilization was reduced to several scattered communities linked by a frail network of poor roads. Along these roads came the merchants, trading in food or supplies or medicine or blasters, and roving bands of freakish muties that set ambushes and raped and killed. And, on occasion, indulged their taste for human flesh.

Best known of the merchants was the man called the Trader. And the most respected, was his first lieutenant, Ryan Cawdor.

RYAN SAT STILL, fighting to steady his breathing. Sweating, he wiped his face, his fingers touching the patch over his left eye. Then he traced the long, puckered scar that ran down the right side of his face, then tugged at the corner of his narrow mouth.

His mouth was dry and he licked his lips. His first firefight back East had occurred when he was twelve. That was nineteen years ago. A skinny kid with a mop of curly black hair, hefting a battered Arma-lite. For the first time, killing a man. Funny how you remembered the first. Remembered the first man you killed. First woman you made love to.

Both times Ryan had been twelve. On a trip into the Appalachians he'd met a web-fingered mutie and blew half his guts away, spilling the loops of greasy intestines into the man's lap. First woman had been a mulatto whore in a bawdy house near Butcher's Creek.

What brought all that back? "Yeah," he whispered, to himself. "Mouth gets dry and your hands get wet. Mebbe should be the other way round."

Hearing a low groan, he looked to one side of the chamber. It was Finnegan. Fat, jolly Finn, with a red stain drying to brown on his hip, where Hennings had bled on him as Finn hauled his friend to safety. Henn lay still, his breathing ragged and harsh, blood still oozing from the ax-cut along his thigh. Hunaker was coming around. She was on her hands and knees, fiercely shaking her head, forcing the clinging darkness from her mind. She sensed Ryan watching her and looked up at him, running her hand through her cropped green hair.

"Hurts like a bastard, don't it, Ryan? Like a fuckin' bastard."

"Yeah," he agreed.

Okie, the tall, good-looking blaster, heaved herself to her feet in a single, fluid movement, cradling her M-16A1 autocarbine, its eleven-inch barrel like a material extension of her own sullen aggression. Ryan noticed that her wounded shoulder had nearly stopped bleeding.

On the other side of the chamber, J. B. Dix wiped the back of his neck. His eyes blinked twice behind wire-rimmed glasses, and he coughed, clearing his throat.

"Not so bad, this time." J.B. was a man of few words.

Next to him, Krysty Wroth stirred. For her, the passage had been worse than usual, and she was doubled over, coughing and retching dryly. Her long red hair, brighter than fire, tumbled to the floor, seeming to move with its own sentient life. Ryan watched her, still prey to his own warring emotions. The girl they'd rescued from muties only a few short weeks ago had managed to affect him as no other woman ever had. With her dazzling green eyes and wonderful body, Krysty had attracted every man on the war wagon. It had seemed utterly logical that she and Ryan should make love.

But only in the last couple of hours had the realization dawned on him that the girl was a mutie. Under extreme stress she could produce a burst of violent muscular energy that was awesome. He still hadn't sorted out how he felt about falling in love with a mutie.

"How's Doc?" he asked, moving unsteadily across the hexagonal room, stooping by the hunched figure of the old man.

Doc was huddled over, his hands clasped between his legs. His cracked boots were smeared with drying mud, and dirt was smeared across the shoulders of his faded frock coat. His battered stovepipe hat was at his side, its crown dented. Tangled gray hair spilled over narrow shoulders. As Ryan nudged him with the toe of his boot, Doc stirred and moaned, his mouth sagging open, showing his peculiarly perfect teeth.

"C'mon, Doc," Ryan said. "Let's find out where you've taken us this time."

"Time, my dear sir," spluttered the old man. "Time is present and also past and, perhaps, even present in the future. Is that where we've jumped?"

"Where?" asked J.B. standing beside Ryan.

"Where what?" replied Doc.

"Leave him be," said Krysty, pulling herself up, straightening her hair. "Poor old bastard's never all here."

The truth was that Doc was never quite anywhere. They'd rescued him some days earlier from a tortured thralldom in a township called Mocsin, southeast of the Darks. The boss of the town had been Jordan Teague, whose corpse now lay somewhere among the smoldering ruins of Mocsin. Ryan and the others had narrowly escaped the enmity of Teague's head sec man, Cort Strasser. Strasser had been Doc's prime tormentor and had used his malign ingenuity to constantly fashion new humiliations for the old-timer.

There was something uncanny about Doc. Despite his frequent ravings and long silences, he seemed to have arcane knowledge of the past. Even the far past, before the wars. But his brain had been so addled by Strasser's cruelty that coherent thought seemed beyond him. Ryan doubted that Doc would ever return to what men called normal.

"Everyone ready? Henn, how's the leg?"

"Not bad, Ryan. I got me another if'n this one buys the farm."

"One leg less to piss down," sniggered Finnegan, ducking Henn's attempt to knock his head off with a roundhouse right.

"The shoulder, Okie?" Ryan asked.

"Stiffening. Never saw what hit me. Arrow, mebbe? I'm fine. We goin' out?"

Ryan moved toward the heavy door to the gateway, but J.B. stopped him. "Best check the weapons. Sooner's better'n later."

J.B. had been the armorer to the Trader for more than nine years, joining the Trader's group about a year after Ryan Cawdor. Despite his mild, almost scholarly appearance, J. B. Dix knew more about armaments than anyone alive. When the world exploded in 2001, every single industrial center vanished in a nuclear cloud. Since then, the manufacture of guns had virtually ceased. But all over the country were hidden stockpiles that had been packed with the requisite tools of war nearly a century ago. And J. B. Dix knew about all of them.

For a couple of minutes the chamber echoed with the clicking of bolts and the testing of springs. Ejected cartridges rattled brassily on the metal floor as the group tested the action of their handguns and rifles.

Ryan drew his panga from its scabbard, felt the honed edge with his thumb, nodded his approval and slid the eighteen-inch blade back out of sight.

Krysty removed her three slim, leaf-bladed throwing knives from the bandolier across her chest, flicking them casually from hand to hand, finding the points of balance.

Only Doc had no weapon. He dusted off his tall hat and attempted to brush his frock coat clean.

"Ready?" said Ryan, getting nods of approval all around. "Then let's go."

The door opened smoothly with the hiss of an air lock. As he led his group into the adjoining room, Ryan heard the faint sound of a distant siren and stopped to listen, but it faded out.

Rectangular and roughly five paces long by three wide, the room was similar to those that he'd seen in other gateways in other redoubts. There was a plastic table on one side and four shelves on the other and nothing else in the room except a polished copper bowl on the table. Hunaker picked the bowl up and peered inside.

"Nothin'. Mebbe somethin' dried at the bottom. Brown crust like blood."

She banged it back down, and it rang like a temple bell, the noise surprisingly loud. Ryan glared at her, and she tried an apologetic half smile. With Hun that was better than nothing.

The far door was shut. If this was like the other redoubts they'd briefly explored, the room beyond would be the main control site for the matter-transmitter complex. Ryan drew his handgun, the weight of the fifteen-shot SIG-Sauer comforting. Around him, the others readied themselves. That was one of the good things about the Trader's training: nobody needed to be told what to do in this sort of situation. You got your finger on the trigger, nerves stretched tight, eyes moving. It was a time when mistakes got made and men died.

One of the things that Ryan liked about the P-226 was its safety. The pistol fired when you pulled the trigger. Not before. Not when you dropped it. He remembered Brecht, the bearded tail gunner from War Wag Two, dropping his old Beretta 92. That was enough to set it off and the bullet hit Karen Mutter, the oldest woman aboard any of the war wags, in her left buttock. Her scream could have shattered crystal at a half mile.

She had been among the dead at Mocsin.

The door opened on a greased track, and Ryan Cawdor stepped through the doorway. It was just like the others. Consoles of whirring instruments, lights flashing red and blue and green. Banks of comps with tape loops that jittered on as they had for a hundred years. It was a great tribute to the technical skill of the engineers before the Chill that these things still functioned after a century of neglect.

He sniffed the air, trying to catch some clue that might prepare him for what lay behind the massive door to the gateway. His limited experience told him it should open on a corridor that was part of a fortress built like some of the stockpiles that they'd found in the last few years.

He flicked on the rad counter in his lapel. It cheeped and muttered quietly, but there was nothing of the fearful crackling that would indicate a hot spot.

"Clean," said J.B., rubbing a finger along the top of one of the consoles, showing it to Ryan.

"Don't spill any dirty blood, Hennings," warned Finnegan, chuckling at his own joke. The tall black limping along at the rear of the party didn't bother to reply.

To the right of the polished metal door was a green lever set at the single word Closed. Cautiously Ryan eased the lever upward toward the word Open.

There was a whisper of gears meshing, and the door began to move sideways. As soon as it had opened a couple of inches, Ryan stopped it. Very carefully he put his good eye to the gap, looking both ways. Sniffing again.

"Anythin'?" asked Okie.

"No. Blank wall. But…I think…seems like I can smell food."

"Food?" Finnegan quickly repeated.

"Yeah, it smells like meat cooking, but it's very faint, maybe from some days ago."

The rad counter was silent, surprising Ryan. What kind of place was this, he wondered, that had virtually no radiation? Had to be a place where there'd been no fighting. Or where they'd used some low-yield weapons with short half-lives.

"Any idea where the fuck we are, Doc?" he asked, leaving the door barely open.

"Not a clue, my dear fellow. Trouble with these jumps. All the control instructions long gone. They took care that the redoubts held nothing, in case any Russkies came sauntering along. All coded and tucked away. All gone?"

"Russkies?" said Krysty Wroth. "Back in Harmony, my Uncle Tyas McNann used to talk to Peter Maritza, about Russkies."

"Russians," J.B. said. "Used to call 'em reds, 'cause they killed so many people. Huge land out west of us beyond where the coast all fell in. Mean bastards—so the old books I read kept sayin' about 'em."

"I'm openin' the door." Ryan pushed the lever all the way up, and the door slid open, revealing a blank wall and a narrow corridor running in either direction as far as they could see. Not that they could see very far; the passage was gently curved, its ends out of sight.

Joining Ryan, they entered the corridor, fanning out with guns ready. He tasted the air again, still catching the elusive but undeniable scent of cooking.

"I can smell it, too," whispered Finnegan. "Good meat stew and fresh bread. That way," he said, pointing to the left.

"Best go that way," said Hennings. "Fat little tub ain't never wrong 'bout food. He'd ride the tongue of the mouth of hell for a mug of broth."

"Left it is," agreed Ryan, leading them off, his bootheels ringing uncomfortably loudly on the stone floor.

This redoubt was different from the others they'd seen. There were no rooms opening off the main corridor, just a long bare passage with a high domed ceiling. At its zenith, lights were deeply recessed behind thick glass. The walls were a restful cream color, unmarked by the passage of the hundred years or so since the place was built.

"See any tracks, Hun?" Ryan asked, after walking a couple of hundred paces.

The girl knelt, placing a hand on the stone, lowering her head until the stubble of her green hair brushed the floor. The others watched. Hunaker was probably the best scout in the group; the Trader had often complimented her about it.

"It's cleaned," she said. "Swept in the last few days by a buggy with fat, soft tires. There's a layer of rubber down here that's real old, like someone's been drivin' the buggy for fuckin' years. No prints."

Ryan led on, every fifty paces or so noticing a slit in the ceiling. Finally he stopped and stared up at one. "Looks like a heavy-armor shield. Drops down to seal off a section."

"Spotted the mini vid cameras?" asked J.B. He pointed with the muzzle of his Steyr 5.6 to a tiny glass bead on a thin metal stem protruding from the wall where it curved sharply into the ceiling.

"Linked to a sonic pickup, I guess," he continued. "Been watchin' us since we left the gateway. Watchin' us now."

"Not now," said Okie, hugging her beloved M-16A1 carbine against her hip, with the stock collapsed, and ripping off a short burst at the camera. Half a dozen 5.56 mm rounds spat from the eleven-inch barrel and exploded into the concrete, pulverizing the little camera. The spent rounds screamed and bounced along the corridor.

"That's brilliant," said Krysty. "Real brilliant."

"Keep your lip sewn up or—" the tall blaster began, turning angrily toward the other girl. But Ryan stepped between them.

"Enough."

"Sure. Take that slut's part, Ryan. Look after your bawdy-house hooker."

"I said *enough*, Okie. There's eight of us here. Either we watch each other's backs or we can all be dead. It's not a fuckin' game, lady."

"Mr. Cawdor!" shouted Doc, pointing with a tremulous finger down the corridor.

It was as he'd guessed. The passage was split into sections, each separated by retractable armor-plated bulkheads. One of them was dropping from the ceiling like an executioner's ax, bisecting the corridor. Before any of them could move, it settled solidly in place on the floor with a metallic clang.

"Bastard!" spat Ryan, spinning around to see precisely what he'd expected. Twenty paces or so in front of them, another door was falling, inexorably sealing them to an exitless part of the complex. And it looked as if the bulkheads were made of some vanadium alloy that would resist their plastic explosives and grenades.

"No bombs," pleaded J.B., looking quickly around the group. "The concussion could kill us."

There was a dreadful moment of tension. Everyone in the party except Krysty and Doc had often put their lives on the line. On the war wags, ambushes and traps were part of everyday life. The best chance of escape was almost always in the first paralyzing breaths. Everyone knew that.

Now all of them moved and turned like caged animals, fingers white on triggers, eyes raking the walls and floor and ceiling for some hint of an escape route. But the only marks that sullied the smooth whiteness were the pockmarks where Okie had wasted the vid camera.

It was a frenetic ballet of nerves. Knowing that everyone was riding the knife edge, Ryan called for calm. "Easy. Easy. Whoever it is, they've got us cold."

A voice reverberated from a hidden speaker, so distorted that it was difficult to tell whether it was male or female, young or old. But the message was clear.

"All dressed up to kill . . . but look who's goin' to die. Guns down, slow and easy. Hands up on heads. You have ten seconds, then I let the gas in. It'll kill you in less'n half a minute."

Ryan spotted another camera near the top of the bulkhead in front of them and guessed the speaker was linked to it. Which, he realized, was a useless bit of information.

"Quickly!" the voice barked, changing then, frighteningly, to a childish whisper. "Do it. Game's done. Ally, ally oxen free. Ally, ally oxen free."

Ryan put his guns on the stone floor and placed his hands on his head. The others followed.

Chapter Two

AFTER THE NUCLEAR HOLOCAUST of 2001, Russia ceased to exist. The U.S.S.R. vanished overnight and, in sixty searing minutes, the purging flames of the brief war that ended all wars destroyed every single Russian city and industrial complex. Every armaments factory and missile base, every port and bridge, was nuked. The destruction was total.

In places—particularly the farthest recesses of the north and east in the devastated Kamchatka Peninsula, in Siberia and the parts of old Russia near North America—the nuclear winter lingered just as in other regions of the globe, the leaden skies and bitter cold had reigned for a generation.

To survive in temperatures that rarely rose above five degrees required a brutal adaptation. The trees of the taiga were destroyed; only a few stunted, mutated pines were left in millions of acres. Most of the wildlife had succumbed as an almost universal death spread across the North. What animal life survived became mutated like the trees.

And the children of the people who survived, many of them were born mutated like the animals.

The peasants in the Russian hamlet of Ozhbar-chik knew little of living. What they understood was how to barely exist. They understood how to maintain the breath in their scrawny bodies on a diet of dried fish and the occasional lucky find of the carcass of a small mammal that the wolves had abandoned. Beyond that, there was watery milk from the village's four rack-boned cows, and an endless diet of potatoes, turnips and other root vegetables. One of the peasants owned a few chickens, and once every few weeks found a tiny egg among the rotting straw.

In these tumbledown hovels, which were scattered along a shallow valley about fifty miles from the sea, there lived thirty-seven men, nineteen women and four children. Only one of the villagers, a man, was older than thirty-five. The grubbing lives of the people of Ozhbarchik were brutish and short.

One of the children of the village, a young boy had the rheumy-eyed, vacant stare and slobbering, sagging mouth of a congenital idiot. His right hand had no thumb, and on his left hand were crammed eleven shrunken, residual digits. Beneath the torn cloth and stinking furs he had two separate and distinct sets of genitalia. One set was male.

One was not.

The group of men surrounding him weren't familiar. A few of them were large men and rode horses, but most of them were small and were astride squat, shaggy ponies. All of them wore layers of fur over their bodies and heavy fur hats halfway over their slanted eyes. Most had rifles slung across their shoulders. Behind them was a train of a dozen pack horses carrying bigger guns and food.

The boy smiled and nodded. Strangers were rare in Ozhbarchik. Strangers meant happiness; he knew that. Sometimes there was music and dancing; he liked that, liked to caper with his ponderous steps, his head swinging low, his hands pawing the air like a mutie polar bear. When he danced like that, his mother and father laughed.

It was good.

The man leading the party of riders was tall, close to six feet. His eyes were almond shaped, with golden irises. His mouth was thick lipped and kindly. Around his forehead he wore a band of beaten silver with a large ruby at its center. His name was Uchitel, and he was nicknamed the Teacher because he was almost the only one in the band who was literate. But that wasn't what made him the leader.

"Boy," he called.

"Yes, master," replied the boy, as he'd been taught, bowing low.

"This is Ozhbarchik?"

"Yes, master."

"There is food here?"

"Yes, master."

Uchitel nodded. "It is good to see such politeness in one so young. Surely the fathers here teach their children well.'' The lad grinned, shuffling his booted feet in the powdery snow. ''They will welcome strangers and will give us food and wine, will they not?''

''Give, master?'' The boy was puzzled. They didn't ''give'' anything to anyone. They sold or traded or bartered. There was little enough for them.

''Yes, boy. Give us all food? Do you not understand that?''

Despite his idiocy, the lad knew when something was wrong. The smile disappeared from his face as he backed slowly away. ''We do not give food, master. No food to give. Poor.''

Uchitel turned in his saddle, nodding sagely to the group's incendiary expert, Pyeka, the Baker—the baker of men.

''This spark of sunlight says that his people are poor, Pyeka.''

''It is sad to be poor, Uchitel.''

''It is truly sad to be poor.'' To the retreating boy, he said, ''Are all poor in your village?''

The stranger's face hadn't changed. There was no anger in the voice, no scowl to the wide mouth. The strange yellow eyes remained fathomless, inscrutable. But something was different. The young boy was so terrified that his bowels loosened and he fouled himself.

''He doesn't answer you, Uchitel,'' called Bochka, the Barrel, a fat man on an equally fat horse.

"No. He must be taught a lesson in manners, after all. But what of these poor? Can we help them seek a road from their poverty?"

The man was making a joke. The boy saw that, because many of the men were laughing. But he hadn't heard him say anything funny. He felt dimly that he ought to go and warn his father and mother about these strangers. But his feet seemed frozen to the ground.

It was the lean figure of Zmeya, the Snake, who answered. "There is one sure cure for the poor, Uchitel."

He reached inside his furs and drew out an oiled pistol—a 9 mm Makarov PM, manufactured in the hundreds of thousands in many state factories before the long winter began. It was a compact, handy automatic with a double-action trigger. The band had discovered a cache of them in a concrete bunker seven months before, and Uchitel had insisted that every member take one. Before that they'd had a variety of Stechkins, TT-33s, Radoms and Walther PPKs. Uchitel saw the value of them all carrying the same handgun, though each still carried his own favorite rifle or machine pistol or carbine.

The boy's eyes opened wider and he began to snivel. Some of the villagers had guns, but the weapons were old and battered, mended with baling wire. He'd never seen anything like this glittering, polished pistol. The slim man tossed it upward so that the dim sun was reflected in the silver stars on each side of the crosshatched butt.

Several of the horsemen drew their guns, laughing as the lad fell to his knees. The front of his breeches was now marked with urine; he'd completely lost control.

Out in the open, among the low scrub of the tundra, the cracks of the handguns sounded surprisingly flat and unmenacing. The first bullet hit the kneeling boy through the right shoulder, knocking him over. Blood gushed from his ragged clothes, staining the snow. A second shot tore through his left thigh, exiting and taking with it a chunk of muscle the size of a man's fist. Blood poured from this gaping wound and the boy screamed, a thin and feeble sound in the wind-washed wasteland.

"He is still poor, Uchitel," yelled Krisa, the Rat, a tiny man with eyes as red as glowing coals. Krisa took careful aim, steadying his right hand with his left, then squeezed the trigger twice.

The first bullet tore into the boy's chest, snapping ribs, exploding the lungs into tatters of torn tissue, sending bright arterial crimson spurting from the gaping mouth. The boy's yelping ceased, and he made a desperate attempt to escape. But the wound in his leg unbalanced him and he fell.

By falling, he put the diminutive Kris off his aim. He had intended to shoot the dying boy again through the center of the chest. But the 9 mm round smashed into the lad's face, breaking his lower jaw and tearing it away on the left so that it hung, hideously lopsided, the row of jagged and broken teeth spilling out with the impact. Continuing, the lead sliced through the boy's tongue and the roof of his mouth, digging deep into the dark caverns of his brain.

The boy kicked in the snow like a rabbit with a broken spine. Watching, the horsemen cheered and laughed; a couple of them made wagers on how long the poor rabbit would last. After fifteen or twenty seconds the corpse lay still, looking oddly shrunken, its blood staining the snow.

Uchitel stood in the stirrups, waved a gloved fist and shouted above the eternal wind, "He is poor no more, my brothers and sisters. Let us go now to his filthy hamlet of Ozhbarchik and help them all to escape from poverty."

As he heeled his black stallion forward, he heard the group laughing. Uchitel smiled, relishing their happiness. In a harsh world, it was good to give pleasure.

The boy's corpse soon stopped bleeding and the wind began to cover it with snow. But not enough to hide it from the scavengers who came creeping from secret places to rend the flesh from the bone.

UCHITEL KNEW that somewhere far to the west of them was a range of mountains, including several volcanoes, and beyond that the ruins of what had been a fine city that he had once visited. Called Yakutsk, it was near the left bank of the Lena River and had been home to over one hundred thousand people. Intercontinental ballistic missile bases near it had sealed its fate in 2001, and the Americans had used "clean" missiles against it, which slaughtered human beings but left buildings more or less intact. But the change in the climate over the next four generations had made a ruins of the city. Uchitel had been there three times, once when he was only fourteen, then twice in his twenties. There he had found old books and had taught himself the skills that allowed him to lead the guerrillas.

He knew how the land had changed. Lakes had appeared and drained. Mountains had sunk and valleys risen. And in many places there were new smoldering volcanoes.

He sniffed the heavy, ugly smell of sulfur that hung in the air. The wind carried the pale yellow tint of the chemical, fouling the high Arctic, making breathing extremely unpleasant.

Angrily he tugged his thick scarf over his mouth and pulled down his fur cap so that only his amber eyes faced the gusting snow. The boy couldn't have been more than a few minutes walk from his home, he judged; these groveling mutant curs in the wilderness never went farther than a mile from their houses. Rarely did you hear of anyone journeying any distance. There might be a merchant, but to catch one alone was as rare as a day without ice. They traveled in armed convoys and there would be little to bring them this far from anything resembling civilization.

In a tavern a hundred miles southwest, a merchant had whispered disturbing news to Uchitel—news that the man had tried at first to sell.

"How much for word of a hunt?" he'd asked, his greasy head to one side, his little eyes blinking with greed.

Uchitel had asked him why he should pay for such news.

"Because of who is the hunter and who is the hunted" was the reply.

Sitting on his horse, waiting while the stragglers in the band crossed the trackless terrain, Uchitel smiled beneath his scarf at the memory of the plump merchant. To prompt the little man, the tall chieftan had taken his left hand in both of his.

Squeezing.

Squeezing until the merchant whimpered and sweat burst from his temples.

Squeezing until blood came around the sides of the purpling fingernails and the man wept to his mother's grave for Uchitel to stop.

Squeezing until his own knuckles grew white with the effort. And the trader told his tale in a stammering rush of tears.

And still squeezing until every finger bone was cracked and splintered, one against the other. Then pushing the crippled man to the floor among the straw and spilled wine and vomit.

"Much farther, Uchitel?" asked Urach, the Doctor, reining his pony alongside Uchitel's. Urach was the only other man in the party who could read and write. But his nickname—it should have been Surgeon—came from his skill with knives.

"No," Uchitel replied, annoyed at having his reverie interrupted. The fat little trader had given him news of a hunt. News that Uchitel had found most unwelcome.

Though the sun appeared intermittently, most of the day was bleak, with flurries of snow reducing visibility. It was bad, but they had all seen much worse. Occasionally a freak tornado came screaming from the north. The wind would be so strong that it would lift a man and his horse together and send them crashing to their death a mile away. Uchitel recalled being in a township to the south when such a storm arose. The buildings, tethered to bedrock with cables of spun metal, held safe. But one of the group, having drunk too much wine, was caught out in the open. The wind destroyed him, splinters of razored ice flaying the clothes from his flesh, then the flesh from his bones.

To the left, Uchitel spotted movement, white against white. He reached for the Kalashnikov AKM

7.62 mm, then saw that the bear was moving away from them in a lumbering, unhurried gait. It could be on its own, or it could be one of a large pack of bears whose tracks they'd spotted a day earlier.

Zmeya saw the first of the little houses, which were so flat in the snow that they were almost invisible. "There," he said, pointing ahead and a little to the left.

Uchitel grinned wolfishly. Night wasn't far off. It would be good to have somewhere to shelter against the lethal drop in temperature. Already he could feel the extra bite in the wind. He lowered the scarf from his nose and mouth, his breath pluming out around him like a bridal veil. Within seconds there was the familiar feeling of his nostril hair freezing, the moisture becoming ice.

Uchitel's band carried enough provisions for a couple of weeks. There was generally the chance of shooting some fresh meat. But best of all was finding a community that would support them for a night or two. Some villages grudgingly consented. Most had to be persuaded. The last time they'd visited Ozhbarchik, more than a year back, there had been trouble and a knifing. Uchitel felt that this time their methods of persuasion might have to be particularly harsh.

At that moment, remembering the words of the

little merchant, he rose in his horned saddle, peering into the snow spume behind them.

There was nothing to be seen.

Nothing, for the time being.

Chapter Three

WITH THE HISS of compressed air, the massive doorway immediately ahead of them began to rise slowly, clearing the corridor. They remained standing still, hands on top of their heads.

"Good," said the disembodied voice from the speaker. "Very good indeed. The Keeper spares you. A sign of anger, and you would have all been cleansed."

None of the eight needed it spelled out. "Cleansed" was just another word for killed or iced or wasted or chilled or blasted or sent to buy the farm.

"You ain't muties?"

It sounded like a question, so Ryan answered it. "No, we're not muties."

"Them women got funny hair. Ain't natural. Green and red. They muties?"

Ryan thought about Krysty. She didn't really look like a mutie at all, despite what he knew of her hidden powers.

"No, none of us is a mutie."

The crackly voice resumed again. "The Keeper says he wants to know how you got in here?"

"Long story," said J. B. Dix.

"Got time. Keeper's got all the time in the world."

"Can we put our hands down?" asked Ryan.

"No. Yes. Yes, the Keeper says yes. Nobody never got in this redoubt. Never in a hundred, never in a thousand, never in a million years. Keeper don't allow it. Doors sealed tight as a bat's ass. No alarms on the outside. Just from the gateway. That how you got in?"

Ryan glanced sideways at J.B. It was a bad situation. The thin, tinny voice sounded crazy. That didn't alter the fact he had them cold. The forces controlling the redoubt would have access to all kinds of sophisticated weaponry. They needed only to shut that bulkhead again and pump in the nerve gas and they'd be dead in seconds. Better to play along.

"Yeah. We come from the Darks. Don't rightly know how or why."

A cackle of laughter. "Not even the Keeper knows 'bout the gateways. You jumped ... where from?"

"The Darks. Used to be called Montana. What else do you want to know?"

"Keeper wants to know everythin', friend. Keeper does know everythin', friend. You say you didn't know where you was comin'?"

"Yeah. Where are we?"

"In good time, friend. Keeper has the redoubt in his charge. Keep it safe. Let no man enter with hate in his heart. You got hate?"

Ryan shook his head. "No. We come in friendship."

Around him he could feel the tension of the others. None of them was very good at waiting.

"Surely shall the lion lay down with the lamb. I have to search the books for word on what to do. Keeper has to take care. Move not, friends. Leave your blasters on the floor. I'll watch. So wait."

"Let's run for it," whispered Okie. She was just behind Ryan.

"Where?" retorted J.B. "Pass that door, and there'll be another."

"Can't just fuckin' wait for the bullet," said Hennings, moving to the side of the passageway and sitting, back against the wall.

"Who do you figure this Keeper is? Some warlord? A baron?"

J.B. shook his head at Ryan's question. "Could be. Sounds old." Lowering his voice, he added, "And crazy as all hell."

They put their guns in a pile and waited, mostly in silence, for about fifteen minutes. Eventually all of them except Okie joined Henn on the floor of the corridor.

"The Keeper has considered. You are people of peace? With hearts full of contrite?"

Ryan didn't know what "contrite" meant, but he nodded anyway. Seemed the best answer. "Yeah."

"You are hungered?"

"Yeah." Finnegan got the answer in first.

"Come forward. Leave your weapons of destruction. You will not need them while under the protection of the Keeper."

"Can't wait to meet him," muttered Hunaker, standing and stretching like a big cat.

Hennings went to retrieve the radio, but the voice from the loudspeaker snapped, "No! Leave that. There is no need to communicate with the chill beyond these walls. None."

"Can hardly reach War Wag One, anyway. Range is only 'bout fifteen miles. Could be way farther off than that." Hennings put the radio back with the blasters and grenades.

Ryan led them through the circular corridor, past several doors in the roof. The smell of cooked food became stronger. Intermittently they passed beneath a tiny, silent vid camera.

"This goddamn place goes on forever," moaned Okie, kicking a wall. Sparks flew from the steel tips of her combat boots.

"Doc? You got any ideas where we might be?" asked Ryan.

Since they'd emerged from the gateway, the old man had been strangely quiet, stalking along, the antiquated hat perched on top of the bony skull. The business of the trap and the creaking voice with its orders hardly seemed to have bothered him at all. Now he started at Ryan's question.

"What was that, my dear Mr. Cawdor? I fear that my thoughts were elsewhere."

"Any idea where we are?"

"In a redoubt, sir."

"We fuckin' know that," sighed Hunaker.

"It is a place of some size, unless I miss my guess. My memory is clouded.... After a jump, I have always been a touch...there were so many."

"How many?"

"Many stockpiles and also many redoubts. Indeed, in places of the blessed land where it was thought attacks might be concentrated, I recall they built some redoubts that were also stockpiles. Perhaps this is such a place."

They'd been walking, by Ryan's calculation, for nearly fifteen minutes, covering more than a mile at their brisk pace.

When they reached a steel barrier, blocking their progress, they stood and stared at it. Finally Ryan stepped forward and looked into the nearest camera.

"I am becoming tired of this. We are all hungry and thirsty and in need of rest. We come in peace. We have laid down our weapons, yet still you treat us like an invadin' enemy."

Even as he spoke, he realized that he had unconsciously slipped into the same form of address as the person behind the screens.

"The Keeper has never seen the like," came the reply, crackling and wheezing. Either the sound reproduction was poor or a decrepit old man was talking. Or both.

"Then let us see this Keeper. Let us talk to him. We are few. This redoubt must hold hundreds of armed men."

A burst of laughter spluttered from the loudspeaker, followed by silence.

J.B. moved closer to Ryan, and whispered, "Could use the plas-ex and run for that gateway."

"Yeah. Get the fuck out of this fireblasted place. Let's..."

He was interrupted by the door ahead of them beginning to slide slowly upward, revealing the legs, then bodies, then heads of three people standing facing them.

"I'll eat my bastard blaster," whispered Okie, shaking her black hair in disbelief.

Two women and a man were spread across the corridor, two paces apart, each holding a gun. Ryan sized them up, trying to hide his bewilderment. He'd expected to see the cream of the redoubt's guards: a squad of uniformed sec men, helmeted and masked, each with a gleaming laser rifle or sonic stunner.

The man at the center of the trio stood a scant five feet tall, Ryan guessed. He was dressed in a bizarre assortment of rags and tawdry finery: a jacket that bore sparkling sequins, leather breeches that were hacked off raggedly above the scrawny knees, and a woman's high-heeled boot on the right foot and a stained shoe of blue canvas on the left. Numerous medals on scraps of iridescent ribbons, jingled from his left breast. A bandolier that crossed his chest contained an extraordinary range of ammunition. Even at a snatched glance Ryan could make out six or seven different calibers.

It was tough to estimate his age. He was so stooped and bent that he might have been ninety. His long white beard was stained amber, seemingly with nicotine, and strands of orange and green ribbons were plaited through it. His hair was streaked silver and gray, and straggled to his shoulders. His face was in shadow, but it was possible to make out a narrow mouth, a hooked nose and deeply set eyes beneath beetling brows.

On the right was a woman of a similar age and garb. Her jacket and leather breeches were so dirty that their original color was indeterminable. She wore a cap, pulled to one side and decorated with cheap glass brooches. She was grinning, showing a picket fence of broken and chipped teeth.

Ryan finally rested his eyes on the other woman. Close to six feet tall, she had natural poise and elegance. Her hair was a tumbling mane of bright gold over a red satin blouse. Her belt had an ornate silver buckle. Her skirt was pale maroon suede—it ended well above the knee—and her legs were encased in high boots of polished crimson leather, the high heels ornamented with tiny silver spurs that tinkled softly as she moved. A pearl-handled pistol hung at her right hip.

Her eyes were a deep summer blue, gazing frankly at Ryan and each of the others in turn. The touch of her eyes was like a caress across Ryan's cheek, and he was astonished at the girl's power. She couldn't have been more than sixteen.

All three of the strangers carried the same weapon and held them with the casual ease of professionals. Yet there was something about them that gave Ryan pause. Their ease was studied, almost as if they'd mastered it from a picture in a book. Real killers had a constant tension to them; they never relaxed.

"Heckler & Koch silenced sub-MG," whispered J.B., at Ryan's elbow.

But Ryan had already recognized the guns. He'd seen odd examples in uncovered stockpiles. The model was the MP-5 SD-2. Loaded, they weighed nearly seven pounds. Not that accurate over any distance, but twenty paces away, as they were now, the trio of guns would rip them apart.

"Greetings from the Keeper of this redoubt, strangers," croaked the old man. "Never have there been such outsiders here."

Ryan was utterly confused. Where were the sentinels? The platoons of armed sec men? Who was this dotard with the two ill-matched women?

"Thank you. Are we welcome here?"

"We think so. The Keeper thinks you are. What are your names?"

"I'm Ryan Cawdor. This is J. B. Dix." The Armorer took off his crumpled fedora and nodded. "Hennings and Finnegan. Lady with the green hair is called Hunaker, and the lady with the red hair's Krysty Wroth. Tall one's Okie."

"What of him?" The barrel of the machine gun swung toward Doc, who was lurking at the rear of the group.

"Name's Doc Tanner. Dr. Theophilus Tanner. I'm pleased to make your acquaintance, sir," he said, bowing deeply, swinging his tall hat behind him. "And you, ladies."

Ryan was thunderstruck. "Tanner? Theophilus Tanner! You said you didn't know your fuckin' name, Doc! How in the...?"

The old man shuffled his feet in embarrassment, like a boy caught with his hand in the cookie jar. He grinned expansively and shrugged. "Guess a door sprang open that I'd thought had closed forever. Just came, like that."

"Theophilus," said Krysty. "What kind of a name is that, Doc?"

"My name, madam. A poor thing, perchance, but mine own." He backed away, mumbling to himself. "How could I have forgotten it? How could I?"

"Day of surprises," said J.B.

If Doc's memory had really returned, then there were many questions that Ryan wanted to ask him. But that would have to wait until later.

"You had best come. That is the invite of the Keeper. There is food."

"Our blasters?" asked Okie.

"Later, my pretty little chick. All things later. First come and eat. There is enough."

For the first time, the old woman spoke, laughing in a bubbling snigger like air rising through molasses. "Oh, but there's plenty for us all for eternity." She seemed likely to choke on her own merriment. "Eternity, or even fuckin' longer!"

The stunted old man made sure his "guests" went ahead of him. The two women stayed behind them on either side, and he stayed right at the back, calling out instructions.

"This place is bigger'n most villes," said Ryan, walking beside Krysty. They walked another nine or ten minutes, moving into a part of the redoubt with side rooms, all with closed doors. Twice they reached junctions, taking first the left fork, and later the right.

"Any ideas, Doc Tanner?" Ryan asked, glancing back over his shoulder.

"Just *Doc* does fine. No. Biggest I've ever seen. I figure there's maybe a stockpile linked. I confess that I have never heard of such a monstrous Gormenghastian pile."

"Got to be hundreds running it," suggested Krysty, but Doc shook his head.

"I beg to differ, Miss Wroth. They were designed to last millenia with no supervision. A child could manage one of these once everything was set and functioning. I recall the malfunction rate was markedly below one percent of one percent of one percent."

Ahead there was yet another barrier.

"Halt. The Keeper commands obedience. Beyond that portal is food and rest for the weary traveler. Not that we've ever had a traveler before, weary or not."

"We can take 'em," whispered Finnegan. "We all got knives. Krysty's got the three throwers. Take 'em all easy as fartin'."

"They'll take half of us. Not good enough," said J.B.

Ryan watched the doddering old man aim a small black remote control device at the top of the closed door. It was obviously a simple sonic switch that activated the opening lock.

"Move forward and enter the demesne of the Keeper of the redoubt."

They stepped through, beneath another raised barrier, and found themselves in a great mall of another century. The floor was a patterned mosaic of soft tiles. At the center of the mall, which was two hundred paces long by a hundred wide, was a glittering fountain shaped from curves of polished metal, with water burbling and chirruping from level to level. And on every side were stores. But stores of a kind that none of them had ever seen even in their wildest dreams.

Ryan looked around, his jaw sagging, his single eye dazzled wherever he stared.

"Blessed Judas Iscariot," he heard Doc whisper. "We've chron-jumped."

But the words meant nothing to Ryan, and he forgot them in the bewildering sights all about them.

"I'll fuck a dead stickie," said Hunaker in amazement.

"The Keeper will allow you to reconnoiter the parameters of the redoubt once you have eaten."

"This must take an army," said Hennings.

The old man cackled. "You think so, black man?"

"We told you our names," said Ryan. "How 'bout yours?"

"This my wife, Rachel," said the old man, pointing to the old woman, who curtsied. "And this is my other wife, Lori. She don't say much. Bein' a dummy, that's why.''

"And where are the others?" asked Krysty.

"Others? Ain't none. We're everybody." He and the old woman giggled.

"Then, where's...who...?" Ryan was lost for words.

The old man had a coughing fit, and it was some seconds before he could speak clearly. He wiped some drooling spittle from his beard. "Me? I'm Quint the Keeper, young man. The Keeper of the redoubt, and my word is law, and the law is death."

Chapter Four

THE BLIND, MEWING CREATURE tied naked to the bed bore little resemblance to a human being.

Once it had been a farmer named Ivan Ivanovich. It had struggled broken-nailed for a pitiful existence in cruel fields of poisonous soil. It had been married to a wife who had died of a bleeding illness eight years back, leaving three squabbling children. Two of them were mutants, with grotesque facial disfigurements. One had a third, soft pineal eye, exposed and raw, weeping constantly in the center of his forehead.

Now there was only darkness.

Not the comfortable darkness of a cold night, with an iron stove glowing with heat and he and his family huddled together under blankets all in one huge bed.

"Not day...not night," he mumbled through his broken teeth. But Ivan Ivanovich couldn't hear his own words, because a sharp file had been thrust into his ears, bursting the delicate eardrums.

There had been no warning. Just the shaggy men, with some devilish women among them, looming out of the driven snow and the fading light. All with guns slung across their shoulders—real guns, not the battered muskets and old bolt-action rifles that the folk of Ozhbarchik could muster.

This band of guerrillas had visited them before. That time the butchers had stolen food and killed a villager who tried to resist them. This time, it seemed, the murderers were bent on killing all the villagers.

Most of the thirty-seven men of Ozhbarchik had fallen in a bloody hail of lead, massacred by the laughing strangers. The nineteen women and three surviving children were seized and held in several of the scattered huts. The cows were each shot with a single bullet through the skull. Ivan's two chickens were chased and caught with much merriment, decapitated, then thrown into a cauldron simmering over an open fire.

Ivan Ivanovich had been the chieftain of Ozhbarchik. His ownership of the pair of fowl had conferred that dubious honor on him. Now he was paying a monstrous price for that honor.

Before his eardrums were pierced, Ivan Ivanovich had heard the leader of the band, named Uchitel, ordering his followers to take what they wanted, roast the animals, eat their fill. He had warned his people to watch for concealed weapons. "A man may dine, yet feel his tripes spilled in his lap," he'd shouted.

There had been screaming; high, thin sounds, as the raiders took their pleasure with the women of the village; Ivan's sister had been taken in front of his eyes by three men at once, with others jostling in a queue behind, their breeches unlaced, and erect, hugely swollen penises thrusting ready.

He'd watched a man fail in his efforts to sodomize a woman then take out his anger by slitting her throat from ear to ear, cursing the dying woman as her blood fountained across his boots.

A huge woman with coarse skin had punched Ivan to the floor, holding him there with a muddied boot, while two other women cut away his clothes with their narrow-bladed knives. They had not been gentle, and his skin was streaming from a dozen shallow slashes from their weapons. They had mocked him as they took and bound him to the rude frame of his own bed, hands and feet pulled painfully apart in a great X. Blood trickled from beneath his broken nails from the tightness of the rawhide cords that bit into the skin at ankle and wrist.

He'd been conscious of the horrors all about him. One of his children had been butchered for refusing to use his tender mouth to pleasure a skinny killer. He'd smelled the scent of a huge fire outside and knew that some of the huts were being used for fuel to roast the slaughtered cattle. Gradually the screaming had died down. None of them had come to hurt him.

Not then. Not at first.

After an hour or so, the leader came to the bed and stared down at him. He wore a long coat made from the skin of a white bear, trimmed with soft sable. His eyes were a curious golden color, his mouth warm and friendly. Around his temples was a band of silver, a ruby at its center.

"This stinking hovel makes me want to vomit, old man. My good brothers and sisters may become sickened from being here. But we shall not stay long."

And he smiled down at Ivan Ivanovich. That was before the pain and the blackness, when Ivan still had a name and knew who he was.

The brutish woman came then, when everyone else was outside. The others called her Bizabraznia, the ugly one. Through the open door Ivan saw the bright flames as they danced and flared, caught the rich taste of the cooking meat, heard the devilish laughter. By then he supposed that everyone in the village was dead.

Bizabraznia, grimacing and farting, lowered her bulk to the side of the bed. He could smell her sour breath, the taint of kvass. The raiders had quickly found the kegs of the sour beer.

"The men enjoy their fucking, little grandfather," she said, reaching out with her broad hand and touching him beneath the chin. He tried to pull away, but the cords held him helpless. She smiled at his efforts, chided him.

Her fingers ran through his straggly beard and the gray hair matted with sweat on his chest. Lower and lower she touched him, bringing her face nearer to his. The little eyes, buried in fat like a suckling pig's, came nearer. Her lips opened and she kissed him, the stubble on her cheeks and chin scraping against his flesh.

For a second, he tried again to resist her foulness, but she gripped his shrunken penis, whispering, "Kiss me sweet, brother, else I'll tug this off your belly easy as wringing a chick's neck. Real sweet kiss, like you and your good wife relish."

Her lips pressed to his, and he fought to respond, closing his eyes against the vileness. Her hand caressed him, rousing him. Her mouth tasted of the stolen food that once belonged to the good people of Ozhbarchik.

She reclined, releasing him, fumbling with her leather breeches, dropping them over her pallid, wrinkled thighs. Bizabraznia belched, putting a hand to her mouth in mock politeness.

"Schchi da kasha pishchna nasha," she laughed.

"The only food is cabbage soup and gruel." Somehow the child's verse was a foul obscenity on her chapped lips, and he nearly threw up. Again he restrained himself, knowing that this monstrous harridan would kill him if he didn't please her.

The woman heaved herself up and squatted over his thighs, grinning, trying to bring him to erection. "Not much for you, is there? Not in the way of a man, eh? There's a good... Something's stirring, I swear. Not much of a fucking worm, but better than...ah."

The ultimate nightmare was that she succeeded. Despite everything that had passed, Ivan Ivanovich became more roused than he had for many impotent years. He thrust up against her, grinding his hips against her muscular buttocks. She reached a gasping climax, accompanied by the cheers of the dozen or so bandits that had come in from the bitterly cold night to watch the show.

Bizabraznia heaved herself off him, depriving him of the small pleasure of his own orgasm, sitting down again with a disgusting sucking sound.

"Please..." he said.

Her eyes narrowed and she slapped him brutally across the face, nearly knocking him unconscious. He could taste his own blood from a cut lip.

"'Please,'" she mocked. "I use you. That's all, you little shit. Honor, for him, isn't it, brothers?" Her appeal brought a chorus of agreement from the men. "If there's time after Uchitel's done with you, grandfather, I might come again and use you some more."

When the leader returned to the hut, the others crept out like beaten curs. Ivan Ivanovich looked up from eyes made puffy with weeping, seeing the great fire from the ruby on Uchitel's silver headband seeming to fill the room. Now that the others were gone, the fear was greater.

"Is there silver in this dung heap, old man?" His voice was courteous, not rough like the rest of the raiders'. "I see you've been hurt." He touched the cuts across Ivan's chest and thighs where the blood had dried. "Tell me about any gold or silver. Or guns. Or more food. Tell me, old man. Come, sing me a song that will make me smile, and you can go free and live."

Ivan's mouth opened and a single word crept out. "Nothing. Nothing, nothing, nothing."

"I am not a common bandit. I have the art of reading and writing, old man. I have books. Books from before the great winter. I have books that show where the towns stood, with pictures of the clothes that men and women wore. Do you hear me? Open your eyes."

The voice snapped at Ivan Ivanovich. It touched the dark places of his mind with a shudder.

Past and present ebbed and flowed.

It was a dream and soon he'd wake. He'd be warm against the rutting body of the little Yevgenia. Despite the cleft palate and the skin ailment that made her face like the scaly back of a fish, she could come closest to stirring him. The memory of the pain was only a shade of the blackness. He'd wake and it would all be done. Even the man Uchitel who...

"Wake up and look at me. Use your eyes." To Ivan, the words were senseless, as was the laugh that followed them. "I tell you I have books and I can read them. Even a book that tells me how to speak with the Americans across the ice river east of here. Think of that. But I talk and you listen. Now you must talk and Uchitel will listen."

"What?"

"The gold and the silver you have hidden. A book of old times, far before the long winter, tells that peasants—filth like you—hoard riches. You pretend to be poor. But you are not. What of that?"

Ivan Ivanovich was delirious, hardly knowing how he forced out a reply. Everything was blurred and shimmering, like objects seen through the glowing heat above a stove.

"Nothing."

"No?"

"Nyet, nyet, nyet."

Uchitel smiled then and stood up. "You will meet Pechal."

"Sorrow?"

"Yes, sorrow. He is well named, grandfather. He takes his only pleasure from torture. You will speak with him."

"But I swear, I know nothing, sir. Please, my lord. Nothing. By Saint Gregory I swear it."

"Swear by all the saints you want. Only the truth about your secret stores will spare your life."

Uchitel didn't truly believe that such a stinking hamlet as Ozhbarchik could possibly have anything worth hiding. But his men liked to dream. Sometimes they had actually discovered little caches of arms or a few antique coins of worthless copper.

The voice at Ivan's elbow was gentle, like the voice of a clerk politely requesting information. "Shall I ask him for his secrets, Uchitel?"

"Yes, Pechal. I'll wait and watch."

Pechal's appearance fitted his voice. He wore gray furs, with matching gauntlets and hood. Most of the band were bearded; he was as clean shaven as Uchitel himself. Pechal, the Sorrow, had pale soft cheeks and a rosebud of a mouth that was permanently pursed in disapproval of the world and its evil. He resembled a priest who had spent all his life in a closed seminary, speaking only of good works and following the pathways of the Lord.

Ivan stared up at him, seeing all of this. Pechal leaned over him, and the old man saw the eyes.

They were like chips of wind-washed agate frozen in the eternal ice of the farthest north.

"Tell me now and all will be well."

"*Nyet*. There is nothing. Please. On my wife's grave, I swear, nothing."

It began.

Gradually Ivan Ivanovich disappeared within the pain of the probing and cutting and rending of his body.

Pechal crooned to him constantly, like a father keeping a baby amused while he bathed it in warm water. At first Ivan's pain had been a light, fluttering thing, like touching a hot iron momentarily or feeling the prick of a needle that hurt a moment, then ceased.

"Tell Pechal of your hoard, grandfather. This is nothing to you. Ah, that made you start, didn't it?"

With a slow delicacy, Pechal forced the point of a knife down beneath a toenail, down to the quick, slowly thrusting and scraping until it seemed to Ivan Ivanovich that the marrow of his bones was being rubbed raw.

"You have your hearing, your sight, your voice. Even this." He touched Ivan's limp penis with the cold edge of a dagger. "You can keep them all, old man. Tell Pechal everything and live."

Nothing.

Pechal lit a tallow candle with a match. Then Ivan felt scorching heat on the inside of his elbows, then behind his knees in the soft crinkled flesh. Ivan smelled his own flesh burning. His body tensing upward, he pulled at the cords so hard that they cut into his bloodied, swollen skin.

From outside came the smell of roasting meat and loud, bellowing laughter. Pechal stopped for a moment and stood, stretching his arms. "It is tiring, this asking of questions, is it not?" he asked the old man. "Spare us both and answer me."

Uchitel was drinking from an earthenware mug of *ryabinovka*, a fiery vodka flavored with ashberries. Muttering something to Pechal, he rose and walked out, leaving the door open so that light from the fires outside the hut capered across the walls.

"I believe you, grandfather," whispered the torturer. "But if I relent, then Uchitel will flay the skin from my living body. I have seen him do it."

Ivan Ivanovich slipped painfully into madness. The agony deepened until he lost touch with it. Pechal pressed hard against Ivan's eyes with the balls of his thumbs, making the old man scream.

"Your eyes pain you. I can stop them hurting. Here."

From a shelf on the far side of the stove, he took a carved box of black powder that Ivanovich used for his ancient musket. Holding the lids open, he piled a neat little heap on each eye. The powder felt gritty, like having specks of sand in his eyes.

"Now?"

"Mercy," sobbed Ivan Ivanovich. He might as well have begged the north wind or the layers of ice that were forming over the corpses of his friends.

He heard, actually *heard* the sizzle of his own eyes burning when the guerrilla touched the candle flame to the black powder. His nostrils were filled with the stench.

When Pechal burst his eardrums, Ivan felt only the stabbing pain. The lack of sound was somehow a relief, as though it was the start of a complete sensory withdrawal from the pain. Cutting the tendons in his jaw, burning his nipples, slicing his genitals from his body, leaving only the weeping, raw wound—none of that registered with the poor creature that had been Ivan Ivanovich. Day and night, hot and cold were gone. After that, it was over.

He still breathed. His heart still pounded desperately. But his mind was dead.

His head rocked from side to side and a toneless, faint whimpering sound was all that came from his peeled lips. Uchitel returned and stood alongside Pechal, looking down emotionlessly at the old man's naked, ravaged body. His cold yellow eyes registered the blood, the raised blisters, the scorched eye sockets, the dreadful mute evidence of the castration.

"You have taken him too far, too fast, Pechal," he said, quietly. "Now he will tell us nothing."

"*Da*, I fear that's true."

Uchitel shook his head. "The meat is nearly cooked, and all the animals are butchered and jointed. We can sleep here tonight and move on in the morning."

"Why not stay here for a week or so? The snows are passing. Every time we move, it is farther north, farther east. Soon we shall be at the sea."

"Yes, Pechal. Soon we shall be at the sea. If your whining continues, then I shall pin you out on the ice for the white bears to feed on."

"But . . ."

The tall, lean man shook his head. "You should learn to hold your tongue, my brother Sorrow, or I will rip it from its roots. You know why we move on."

"What the merchant told you?"

"Yes. Now, take this offal out and slit its throat. I am tired, Pechal."

"Did . . . ?"

"What? You are making me weary, brother."

Despite the chilling note of warning, the other man continued. "Did he say where they were? Or how far behind us?"

For a moment, Uchitel stared at him in silence, oblivious of the dying man on the bed behind him.

"Pechal . . . the merchant said he had heard that there was a band of militia hunting us down."

"But did he say where?"

"They were bastard whores' sons, spawned in middens, from the port of Magadan, where, they say, there are houses and many stores and mongrel codsuckers who sit with their thumbs buried in their own asses while they send their puppies on horseback to hunt down men such as you and I, my brother. He said that they had heard we robbed and plundered and raped and burned and slaughtered. His very words, from what I recall of his blubbering. This so-called *government* that believes in some *party*..."

He spat out the two words as if they soiled his lips.

Pechal nodded. "And they will chase us down. Then we shall kill them." He clenched his hand, soft as a woman's, yet with long, curved nails of horn.

"Fool."

"What?"

"You are a fool. These will not be puking peasants like this old shit here on the bed. They will have good guns. No. It is best that we run."

Bizabraznia came staggering in, beer running down her chins, over her open blouse, trickling across her huge, veined breasts. In one hand she held a great smoking haunch of meat, the outside charred and black, blood leaking from its center.

She sniggered at Ivan Ivanovich. "Can I have some sport with him?"

"No. Pechal will cut his neck open outside, and then I can get some sleep. We must all sleep. We have a dawn start tomorrow."

"Then we run from these militia boys, eh?"

Uchitel nodded. "Aye. Lead them far enough, and they'll give up the chase. Then we can return to our hunting grounds once more."

"Where do we run?" asked Urach, standing in the doorway.

"That way," replied Uchitel, pointing east.

"There is nothing there but the frozen sea."

He smiled. "We shall cross it where the strait is narrowest, no more than ninety kilometers wide."

"To the other side?" said Urach, wonderingly.

"Yes, brother. On the morrow we head for America."

Chapter Five

"COULD FUCKIN' STAY HERE forever," said Hunaker on their third day in the huge redoubt.

It was more than just a redoubt. J. B. Dix and Ryan Cawdor had twice revisited the gateway, making sure of the route in case they needed it. They had also drawn a plan of the labyrinthine, rambling corridors, readying themselves for any eventuality. Near the gateway, high on a wall, they'd seen a small notice like the one they'd seen in the redoubt in the Darks: Entry Absolutely Forbidden To All But B12 Cleared Personnel. Mat-Trans.

The red paint was as bright as if it had only been lettered a day ago.

The place, with its incorporated stockpile, was the biggest building that Ryan Cawdor had ever laid eyes on. It was bigger by far than any ville he'd seen, vastly more imposing than any barony out East. The stockpile alone was more than a mile in length and a quarter-mile in breadth, with a maze of interconnecting passages and storerooms, reminding him of pictures he'd once seen in some old, crumbling mags from before the Chill.

It reminded him of what had once been called a "shopping mall."

During the three days, Ryan ordered his party to station themselves anywhere they could in the redoubt. Quint and his wives, Rachel and Lori, kept mainly to themselves, eating in their own quarters.

Ryan's group had their own dormitory: a long room with forty beds, each with a locker. There were showers and latrine facilities, a dining room and a kitchen, with all the plates and pots and cutlery they could need. It was obvious that the place had been designed as a post-holocaust living-space for a couple of hundred people. The air-conditioning kept everything free from dust and dirt.

Most of the complex was open to them, though Quint warned them against trying to force open any locked doors.

"Keeper wouldn't like that," he'd quavered.

Their relationship was odd. Quint and his women, who went everywhere with their Heckler & Koch sub-MGs, made no objection when Ryan and his party retrieved their weapons. If they'd wanted, they could have iced the Keeper and both his wives. Okie and Finnegan wanted to do this, but Ryan and J.B. opposed them.

"No reason. They don't seem a threat. Watch 'em carefully. Could be useful." As ever, the Armorer was brief and to the point.

As far as they could determine, there were only two entrances to the redoubt. One was a huge vanadium-steel doorway like the one back in the Darks, but without a manual control on the inside. Ryan believed it had never been opened since the long winter. It possessed no windows or ob slits anywhere.

One important thing happened during those three days.

J. B. Dix managed to find out where the redoubt was. After what Doc had said to them about complexes containing both a stockpile and a redoubt having been built in strategic locations, it wasn't too much of a surprise.

Near a small exit was a room that held some charts. Cohn, the navigator whom they'd left in charge of War Wag One, would have given his right arm for them. They were the best-preserved maps that any of them had ever seen. Though they were frail and tended to crack when they were unfolded, their colors were unfaded. Since Quint wasn't around, J.B. took several and stuffed them in his pack.

One map, which was pinned to a corkboard, showed the area around the redoubt in considerable detail, and Ryan and J.B. studied it with interest.

"Alaska," said the Armorer.

"Yeah," agreed Ryan. "That's where Fairbanks was. And Anchorage. That's the strait. Heard some talk years ago that it was all frozen over here. The winter never moved after the Chill. And there, on the left side, a few miles west..."

"Russia," said J.B., nodding.

"Close," said Ryan.

MEMBERS OF THE GROUP spent time in ways that interested them, sometimes alone, sometimes in pairs or threes.

Ryan was with J.B. a lot, and with Krysty Wroth the rest of the time. In the hectic days since they'd first made love, it seemed as if an eternity had come and gone. Now, at last, they found some hours to be alone together.

There was a whole suite of rooms filled with weights, rowing equipment, a small swimming pool, exercise cycles and a whirlpool bath with the name Jacuzzi on it. Green metal lockers held clothes, towels, leotards, trunks and wraps. Krysty peeled off her stained overalls and pulled on a tight red leotard with white flashes down the arms. Ryan smiled at her enthusiasm.

"Get stripped for action," she called, sitting astride the white saddle of a stationary bike, tucking her bare feet under the straps and beginning to pedal.

The temperature throughout the redoubt and stockpile was sixty degrees. Monitors on a small console in the living quarters showed that outside it was an average of minus forty during the day and minus ninety during the night. A driving northerly wind that sometimes exceeded a hundred miles an hour made it likely that an unprotected human would freeze to death within minutes. Even with the best thermals on, at night or when the wind rose, life would be precarious after more than a couple of hours in the open.

Ryan peeled off his favorite long coat, with its white fur trim, and put it carefully on the padded floor. The SIG-Sauer P-226 9 mm and the three spare ammo packs followed; then the LAPA 5.56 mm and the heavy steel panga, its eighteen-inch blade sheathed in soft, oiled leather. Finally he took his white scarf of fine silk from around his neck and put it neatly by the weapons. It made a soft clunking sound. Hearing the noise, Krysty looked curiously at him.

"What's in that, Ryan?"

"In the scarf?"

"Yeah."

"Couple of bits of lead."

She paused in her frantic pedaling. "What's that for, Ryan?"

He shook his head. "Mebbe one day I'll tell you. Mebbe one day I'll show you."

He peeled his coveralls and his thermal vest and pants, laying them by the weapons. Stripped, he was aware of his own stink.

"Fireblast!" he exclaimed.

"What?"

"I smell like a stickie's armpit. Got to have a bath and clean up. Never noticed it."

"Use that bath. Looks good. There's instructions on the side."

"Pity those that can't read," he said, moving to the large oval tub. Krysty watched him, admiring the lean body, with the ridged walls of muscles across the stomach, the tightness of the thighs and the hardness of the chest and shoulders.

"You need a shave as well," she said.

"Mebbe later."

"You know that Quint can't read."

"What?" he straightened up, unable to hide his surprise. "He's the Keeper."

"Yeah." She stopped pedaling and leaned forward, breathing hard. "This bastard machine's not up to some real action. It's fallin' apart."

"Not that amazin', love. It must be as old as everythin' else in this redoubt."

Following the printed instructions, Ryan turned on the Jacuzzi and started filling it with hot water. "You sure Quint can't read?" he asked.

"Certain."

"How?"

"He told me."

"When?"

"Turn that tap farther. The water's not coming fast enough."

Ryan did as she suggested. As he knelt, he was aware of Krysty moving behind him. He didn't turn his head, knowing that she was on his blind side.

There was the breath of material falling softly to the floor. She leaned over him, her long rich crimson hair brushing against his nakedness, caressing him with infinitely soft movements. The touch was enough to arouse him, and she giggled in his ear, reaching over his shoulder with a long arm, her fingers rubbing his chest.

"Krysty," Ryan closed his good eye for a moment, relishing the contact. He swallowed hard, fighting to control his breathing.

"Yeah?"

"When did Quint say he couldn't read?"

"Yesterday. He took me to see that door to the outside. Said there was a whole mess of fuckin' wicked mutie dwarfs out there. That's what he said. They wait. Been waitin' for a hundred years. He talked about being the Keeper. Said that everythin' he knew, he'd learned from his father, who was Keeper before him."

The bath was three-quarters full. The woman knelt behind Ryan, her arms around him, her breasts pressed against his muscular back so that he could feel her hard nipples. She was holding him with one hand, rubbing slowly up and down while, with her other hand, she traced the delicate lace of scars across his shoulders. And all the time her sentient hair was stroking him.

"His father?"

"Yeah, Ryan. Keeper before him. And his father's father was Keeper before that."

"But why's there only three of 'em left? The muties get 'em?"

"Didn't say. Ryan?"

There was a change in her voice, and he finally turned around to look into her face, feeling for a split second as if he might drown in the green depths of her eyes.

"What, Krysty?"

"Muties, Ryan."

He nodded. "I'm not goin' to fuck around, Krysty, and pretend I don't know what you mean. I do know."

She sat back, drawing her long legs up, folding her arms around them, resting her chin on her knees. Her marvelous hair tumbled across her shoulders, coyly covering her breasts.

"Now's the time for this, Ryan. We've known each other a short while. We made love—or we fucked. I thought it was makin' love. You?"

"Yeah, Krysty. I didn't think we were fuckin'. I thought we..."

"That's good. Now, you know I'm a mutie."

"Not—" But she interrupted him.

"Turn off the tap, or we'll flood the bastard redoubt in hot water."

"There. Look, there's somethin' funny about your hair. Like it moves some."

"Some. My mother was Mother Sonja, and the good and bad things about me come from her. She had the power, Ryan. Real power. Gave some to me—some by birthing me, some by teaching me."

"Was she . . . a mutie?"

"More than me. She could make her hair grow long and lift things with it. I saw her do it when I was little. She got older and didn't or couldn't do it anymore. My hair moves a little. Mainly when I'm happy or when I'm . . ." She grinned suddenly, lifting her face, dazzling him with her beauty. "I guess you noticed that, Ryan. And my hair hurts when it's pulled or caught. Or cut."

"That all?"

The washer on one of the taps in the whirlpool bath had rotted, and the water dripped steadily. Ryan watched it, conscious that he was beginning to feel cold.

"No. You know that I've escaped twice with my wrists tied?"

"And you damn near broke the handle on the main door to the redoubt in the Darks."

"Yeah, I did. That's kind of a mutation. But it's more what I meant by Mother Sonja's teaching me things. She taught me how to do that."

"What?"

She looked down again. "It's a sort of focusing, a concentrating on how I feel. It's hard and it tires me some. I call on the Earth Mother, and she comes to help me."

"Just how strong are you?" asked Ryan, still naked, standing and moving around the exercise room, conscious that his erection had vanished and that his penis now slapped limply against his thigh as he walked.

"I don't know. I tried all I could on that door. Our lives were in danger. The effort nearly killed me. I nearly puked my guts up."

In one corner, stacked on a chrome steel rack, there was a bar and a pile of weights. Ryan removed the collars and slid on some of the heavy discs, then replaced the collars and tightened the butterfly screws.

"There are now one hundred and fifty pounds on each side. I figure it's about my top. Can you lift that?"

"Not now." She rose and moved gracefully toward him. Her body was in marvelous condition, like a top fighter.

"But, if you called...on the Earth Mother, could you then?"

"Yes." There wasn't a hint of doubt in her voice as she looked at the equivalent of the weight of two grown men on the smooth bar. "But you first, Ryan. Press that above your head and . . ."

"And what?"

"Do it and see."

"I don't usually lift things with my cock sticking out like this," he muttered, stooping in front of the weights.

"Hanging out, Ryan," she corrected, with a wicked smile.

Ryan waited, gathering his concentration, flexing his fingers around the cool metal. He closed his eye, focusing all his energy on lifting the bar. Six deep, slow breaths, then the explosive whoosh of effort. Feeling the strain at the small of his back and across his chest and shoulders, he lifted the bar from the rack. Ryan Cawdor didn't look that heavily muscled, but his wiry body was in excellent condition. A man didn't get to ride and fight with the Trader for ten years by being soft and flabby.

"Very good," she said, clapping as the weights rose slowly but steadily to chest level, then with an extra boost, above Ryan's head. The tendons in his arms stood out like cords as he held it there, his face suffused with blood. He managed a wink at the girl before he lowered the bar to the floor with a thump.

"Now you," he panted.

"Give me a minute to ready myself."

Krysty began to take deep breaths, her breasts rising and falling as Ryan watched with interest. Her legs were slightly apart, the triangle of brilliant scarlet pubic hair masking her sex. The muscles across the front of her thighs rippled and danced, and he could see the fluttering of her stomach. Her eyes were closed, and her lips moved. In the silence he heard her whisper.

"Now, Mother of Earth, give me, I beg, the power to do that which is right. Let me render no evil. Give your daughter the power, the power, the power..." she chanted, the sound barely carrying to Ryan, three paces away. He stared at her face, seeing it transformed into a mask of carved bone, the planes of her cheeks shifted by an almost unbearable tension.

Krysty stepped to the bar and bent in front of it, her tumbling hair hiding the weights for a moment. She gripped the bar with both hands and then straightened, hefting it above her head in a single, flowing motion.

Ryan's jaw dropped. He'd seen some amazing sights before, but nothing to compare with the way the three-hundred-pound set of weights *floated* up. There was no other word for it. Nor did the girl show any strain now that the deed was done. She held it above her head, her eyes half-open, her mouth sagging, a thread of spittle hanging from the corner of her lips, almost as if she'd fallen into a trance.

"Thanks, Earth Mother," she whispered, then let the weights fall to the floor with a great crash. She staggered and nearly fell, putting her hand to her forehead. But before he could help her, she had straightened, smiling.

"Krysty, are . . . ?"

"I'm fine. Bit tired. Always am. Shouldn't have done that. Showing off is not what the power's for."

"It looked like it was no heavier than a fistful of air."

"Yeah."

"How much . . . heavier could you have lifted?"

She shook her head. "The power of the Earth Mother isn't like that. It's what I want. If there were a buggy turned over on top of you, I could maybe lift it, maybe not."

They stood in silence, looking at each other. Krysty spoke first, eyes locked to Ryan's face.

"There. Now you know what sort of mutie I am."

"Yeah. Now I know. But I think I knew before."

"Now what?"

He stepped close, lowering his head to kiss her softly on the lips, tasting her sweat, putting his arms around her, feeling the way she shuddered with the raw tension. Her breasts pushed insistently against his chest, and her hair rustled on his skin.

"Now I want to get in that fuckin' big bath and make love to you for the rest of the day," said Ryan.

"It doesn't matter, me bein' a mutie?"

"Not unless you use your Earth Mother power when I'm inside you and crush me to pulp."

"Don't joke about it, Ryan."

"Sorry."

She kissed him again, her tongue snaking over his teeth. Her right hand crept down over his stomach, touching the curling tendrils of hair.

His response was instantaneous.

"That's nice," she whispered. "Stickin' out, not hangin' out."

Krysty led Ryan to the whirlpool bath. The water was still hot, and she pressed a violet-colored button to mix in some scented foam, making the exercise room smell like a meadow in summer. A square black button made the water churn and swirl. Great cascades of bubbles burst all around Ryan as he lowered himself cautiously into the bath.

"Nice?" she asked.

"Not bad," he replied, offering a hand to help her step in beside him. There was a ledge around the side of the bath and they sat together on it, the water only a few inches over their laps.

Krysty, her back to him, lowered herself carefully into the water while he caressed her from behind. "Oh, yes. Yes, Ryan, that's great. Not too fast."

Ryan reached around, feeling her nipples move against his palm. His right hand delved lower and deeper, under the water, between her parted thighs, found the tiny bud of flesh that nestled there. Rolling it between his finger and thumb, he enjoyed hearing the girl moan. It became swollen and she leaned her head back, half turning and nipping at the skin of his shoulder, drawing a ruby bead of blood. Gasping she removed his hand from between her legs, then gripped his rigid penis and quickly guided it into her body.

Krysty had extraordinary control over all her muscles, tightening herself about him, squeezing his penis, bringing him toward a raging orgasm.

Though he tried to hold back for her, the girl's skill was too much for Ryan, and he felt himself bursting inside her. But he stayed hard long enough for her to ride him to her own climax.

All around them the scented water continued to bubble noisily. Still sitting on his lap, Krysty kissed him tenderly on the cheek. "Good. Thanks, Ryan."

"It was real good." He paused. "Krysty... Oh, fireblast! Thanks."

After a while they made love once again in the whirlpool bath, then finally got out, dripping water everywhere.

"Should get some clean clothes, Ryan," she suggested.

"Yeah. Tomorrow let's go to the store and find us some."

They dressed in their old gear, making sure their weapons were in place. Krysty, ready before him, looked around the big exercise room, taking in the equipment and the mirrors. The bath was loudly draining.

"Look."

"What is it?"

"The fuckin' spyin' old bastard." She stooped to pick up a length of ragged green ribbon from the floor near the door.

The kind of ribbon that Quint, the Keeper of the redoubt, wore braided in his straggly gray beard.

Chapter Six

"How do the wolves survive, Uchitel?" asked Bochka, the Barrel, astride the largest horse in the party.

"They eat the weak."

"If there are no weak, brother?"

Uchitel peered through the gap between his hood and the scarf around his nose and mouth. "Then they eat each other, Bochka." Raising his voice so the others could hear him, he added, "And if we fall on evil times and must devour each other, I take the leader's right of roasting Bochka all for myself."

A ripple of laughter ran back along the column until it vanished in the murk of wind-blown snow. Since the raiders had left Ozhbarchik two days back, the weather had been deteriorating. Three times Uchitel had ordered emergency shelters to be dug in the packed snow; they used the long-bladed saws that they carried for just such a purpose. It took less than five minutes to throw up a wall of large snow bricks six feet high to protect them all from the lethal wind.

During the rare calms, Uchitel had gazed back, trying to spot any sign of pursuit. Away to the north, he could make out the smoke-tipped cone of one of the many new volcanoes that had appeared at the time of the wars. The snow around it was tinted gold from the sulfur fumes, and there was no sign of any living thing in all that dreadful wilderness. Nothing except the huge mutated white bears that occasionally loomed from the blizzard, threatening the column.

The bears…and the wolves—lean gray shapes with slavering jaws and thrusting muzzles, slinking at the corners of a man's vision. Several times over the years they had lost men to the wolves. It was one of the reasons that everyone feared becoming a straggler.

Only the day before a man had gotten left behind. It had happened to Nul, a quiet, gray-haired man whose nickname was Zero because it often seemed as though he wasn't there. His pony had stumbled over a twisted piece of metal; it was a large mortar shell with tail fins intact, a relic of the missile testing that had once occurred in that area, which was just across the frozen expanse of the Bering Strait from North America. A deep gash in the pony's right foreleg had exposed the tendons, making the pony limp badly. Nul knew the rules as well as anyone. Move slower than the group, and you stayed behind. But there was always a chance of catching up. A man riding alone moved farther and faster than a party.

There was always a chance of catching up again. All he'd have to do was stay alive.

"FUCKING BASTARD! Cocksucking shit-swallowing bastard fucker!"

Nul punched the stumbling pony on the side of the head, making it stagger and nearly fall again. Blood was drying on the streaked flanks where he'd lashed the pony with the buckle end of his belt. He'd hoped that by now he'd be rejoining the band. But the shaggy animal seemed to go slower and slower. Now darkness was less than an hour off, and the band was at least five kilometers ahead. If Uchitel persisted with his plan to cross the ice and invade what had once been America, they could begin crossing the strait in less than a week, maybe in only four or five days. At this rate, Nul figured he'd be more than a day behind by the time they reached the strait.

It was time to stop, build a shelter and get a fire going. Their pyrotabs were often the difference between living and dying. Once lit, one of them would generate enough heat to burn brightly for three hours. Nul had about forty of them in his saddlebags.

That should be enough. If he didn't catch up with the others before they crossed the ice, then he might as well kiss the barrel of the 9 mm Makarov goodbye.

URACH SQUATTED BY HIS LEADER in the lee of the big snow wall. The flames of the fires fought bravely against the swirling sleet. From beyond the circle of light, they heard the keening of the wolves.

"Feedin' on Nul?" he said.

"That's the cry of hunger. When that stops, then maybe they will have found Nul."

"Britva will lose toes after falling through that pool this morning."

"He can use his own razor. It'll teach the imbecile a lesson. Trying to gallop when there is no trail! There may even be live mines this close to the ocean. I have read how they sowed these hills. MZDs and AKSs all over the place."

"What if the Americans are waiting for us, Uchitel? Then . . . ?"

The reply was a silent smile.

"You think there is no danger?" asked Urach, holding out his hands to the flames.

"I know there is no danger. If they were a powerful country, do you not think they would have overrun this land by now?"

"I suppose . . ."

"Of course. Brother, go and fetch me some of that fine meat we took from that dung heap of a village. I am hungered." Then, as Urach was leaving, Uchitel added, "The Communists have gone from this country, Urach. And the Fascists have gone from over there." He pointed to the east. "They have lost, as they always will. Only we remain. As we always will.''

And he began to laugh.

THE PONY WAS GROWING weaker rather than stronger. It was impossible to ride it, and Nul plodded alongside, cursing in an endless monotone. Like Uchitel, he carried a Kalashnikov AKM and every couple of hours he was forced to fire off a short burst to chase a pack of wolves away.

But they returned, circling closer, bellies low to the ground, their gray-white coats melding with the sulfur-stained ice.

The snow had eased, and the wind had also died down. At least he was no longer in immediate danger of freezing to death. The middle-aged man trudged relentlessly eastward, his face set to the ground, one foot following the other, trailing the rest of the party. Every step left him a little farther behind.

Apart from checking the endlessly weaving pattern of the wolves, Nul never looked back.

HIGH CLIFFS stood like jagged teeth above the packed gray-green ice of the Bering Strait. The sea was covered in a dense mist, overlaid with volcanic fumes. The air was heavy and caught at the back of the throat, producing coughs and reddened eyes.

Somewhere beyond them was what had once been called Alaska. Now it had no name at all.

In the year 2000, half a million people had been scattered over the six hundred thousand square miles of this inhospitable land. Now there were less than a couple of thousand people in the whole barren waste.

To Uchitel and his band, the country that lay hidden in the acrid fog was the promised land, containing legendary treasures and riches. The books all said so.

"We go that way, Narodniki," shouted Uchitel, waving his Kalashnikov above his head like a crusader's sword.

There was a bellow of support from the men and women at his heels, the Narodniki.

Uchitel had found the name in the ruins of what had been the central library of the Communist Party amid the wreckage of nuked Yakutsk. He had come across a passage about the populist movement in old Russia. Over two hundred years before, in the late eighteen hundreds, there were terrorist and guerrilla organizations with names like Black Repartition, and Land and Liberty. But the parent of them all was the Narodniki.

It was a name that came to mean terror and blood, a name that appealed to the dark side of Uchitel's nature, which truly had no light side.

"We camp here in the cleft of the rocks that will keep us from the worst of the wind." Above him there was a deafening crack of thunder that made some of the ponies rear and whinny. There was a searing glow of deepest purple from chem clouds that raced hundreds of miles high.

"And tomorrow?" asked Bizabraznia, lashing at her horse with a whip of braided wires.

"Down there, and across into the land of the brave and the home of many, many dead."

NUL WAS FEELING HAPPIER. The pony's fetlock was mending, and in the last twenty-four hours he'd made better time than he had for days. A biting fog had come down from the direction of the icy sea, making progress difficult, but from the fog's salty taste, he guessed that he couldn't be too far off.

The dried beef was lasting well. In one of the huts in Ozhbarchik he'd found some delicious *golubtsy* and had taken enough to last him weeks. The thought of the food safely wrapped in his bag made him hungry, and he reached in, taking one of the cabbage rolls stuffed with fried turnip, biting voraciously into it. The jolting of the pony made him choke on a mouthful. Cursing at the animal, tugging brutally at the reins, he brought it to a dead stop.

"Better," he said, his voice muffled by the food. The fog had drifted away to the south, and visibility was unusually good. He stood in the stirrups, wondering whether he might make out the rest of the Narodniki.

UCHITEL URGED his stallion on. The sea cliffs of Alaska were towering ahead of them, snow tipped, only a hundred paces away. Birds resembling gray gulls, but with a vastly larger wingspan, circled and wheeled from their eyries, their echoing cries like the moaning of long-drowned sailors.

Behind him in single file, came twenty-eight men and women, their horses advancing through the crumpled sheets of jagged ice, watching for the softer contours and crystalline outcrops that might hide gaps in the surface and for hidden crevasses through which a man and horse might easily slide, vanishing completely and irrevocably into the sucking waters.

For the hundredth time that day, Uchitel turned in his saddle, feeling a crick in his neck from continually looking back. Once they were across, they would be safe. He had never heard any legend or read any account of any Russian crossing this narrow shifting neck of ice. If it were true that they were being pursued, then the land ahead of them promised safety.

NUL RAISED THE LAST MOUTHFUL of the *golubtsy* to his lips.

Then he was lying on his back in the trampled snow, staring blankly up at the dull sky.

There had been no sense of time passing. No sense of falling.

No pain.

The only feeling was shock; a sensation that someone had managed to creep up unseen and strike him in the middle of the chest with a huge mallet. He was aware that his feet were kicking and twitching. It felt odd, as though his feet belonged to someone else. With gloves that seemed to be filled with iron, Nul carefully touched the numb center where the hammerblow had come.

He suddenly felt very cold.

A full fourteen hundred paces to the southwest, the tall sniper lowered the Samozaridnyia Vintovka Dragunova rifle. The rimmed 7.62 mm bullet had done its work. Through the PSO-1 telescopic sight he'd seen it rip explosively into the target's chest. The man wasn't going to move very far with a wound like that.

"Good shooting, Corporal Solomentsov. An extra ration of food this month from the grateful party."

The speaker was about thirty, with a long, drooping mustache that hid a pockmarked chin. He stood five inches below six feet and wore a gray uniform of thick material, with long boots of tanned hide. Removing his high fur cap, which bore a single silver circle at the front, he revealed a totally bald head.

"Thank you, Major Zimyanin," said Solomentsov, giving a click of his heels and a sharp bow.

"Holster the Dragunuv rifle, Corporal. You know what ice can do to the sight. Last time you left it uncovered the frost cracked the bulb of the reticle lamp."

"Yes, Major," the corporal replied, taking the long gun and pulling a cloth shroud over the neat sight.

"And send Tracker Aliev to me."

The tracker was less than five feet tall, with the slanted eyes that revealed his heritage. He had the waddling gait of a Mongolian who'd spent most of his life astride a barrel-chested pony. A thick woollen scarf was wrapped about the lower part of his olive-skinned face.

"Aliev, do they still move on toward the sea? Be sure."

The rest of the hundred-strong militia unit kept well clear of the tracker. Some of them crossed themselves when they went near him. His skill at scenting the enemy was so developed that there were those who said he was a witch. As he approached the head of the column, past the depression where Solomentsov had knelt to fire, he unwound his scarf. Though Major Zimyanin had seen him many times, he still fought hard to restrain a shudder.

The nukes used by the Americans in this part of once-mighty Russia had been awesome in their power. Aliev came from a family that had always lived near the Kamchatka Peninsula, and his face was the stigma of his background.

Most of the lower jaw was missing. Where the nose should have been, there was only a large hole fringed with damp pink tissue like rotting lace. The mouth gaped, with a few yellowed teeth left jutting crookedly from the upper jaw. Aliev had no way of closing his mouth, and all food had to be sucked into his gullet.

Across the dark cavern of his nasal orifice, Aliev had a veil of crumpled skin as thin as the wing of a moth. It moved raggedly in and out in time with his raucous breathing. To stand close was to inhale the odors from the entrance of hell, as Aliev only accepted meat that was rotting and crawling with larvae. He would bury his snout in it and devour it ravenously and noisily.

Now he dropped to his hands and knees, closing his eyes, laying his nose to the snow, sniffing. The others watched from a distance, each man holding the muzzle of his horse to quiet it.

Then, as he had a thousand times, Zimyanin wished that he could be transferred to a militia unit far, far to the west. There they had petroleum in some quantity and trucks. He knew because he had seen pictures of them. Soon, he was told, his cavalry would be given trucks. He had heard it several times from his superiors in the last three years. If the party told you something was true, then it was.

"Well?"

The face turned to him, and he nearly vomited at the nauseous panting, sniffing noise that Aliev made in his eagerness.

The brutish head nodded.

Aliev was a wonderful tracker, but he had drawbacks. Apart from the horrific look of the man, he could neither speak nor read or write, which made communication difficult and taught others to avoid unnecessary questions.

"The same ones? Yes. How many days gone? Five? Four? Four. Good." He gestured with a gloved hand for the creature to return to his place in the patrol.

Four days' journey ahead of them, twenty-eight men and women seemed to be preparing to cross the strait and move into what had been America. Zimyanin's heart thrilled in his chest. He knew that no unit of the party's militia had ever been this close to the enemy's land. They could not refuse him promotion if he... But this was leaping a wall before he had even mounted his horse. Nobody would applaud the singer just for clearing his throat.

But to catch and destroy the band of slaughtering butchers ahead would be so good. He had been trailing Uchitel and his marauders for weeks now, even closing in at times. But if they crossed the ice river, then his band of militia might be seen. Perhaps a camp for a day?

Perhaps the body of the man they'd just shot would yield a clue. Zimyanin's head was becoming cold so he replaced his fur cap and walked thoughtfully toward his horse. There was much to think about.

CONFUSED, NUL PULLED OFF his gauntlets and again felt the numb patch in the middle of his chest. He felt chilled, but his fingers encountered a sticky wet warmth. Disbelievingly, he painfully held his hand in front of his eyes. It was dripping with blood, as though it had been thrust into the belly of a slaughtered beast.

"Is this . . . ?" But his words faded.

As he lay on his side, his eyes caught the great lake of crimson growing around him. The numbness was sliding away and there was a dull ache. He touched himself again, and his fingers could feel the brittle sharpness of shattered ribs.

He could dimly make out a group of people. At least a mile away, they were mere dots against the blurring whiteness. "Uchitel . . . ?" he said. It was good that friends came to watch you. Even that heartless bastard Uchitel. He'd come back for him.

UCHITEL'S HORSE galloped off the jagged edges of the sea ice onto the wind-swept boulders of the beach. "I claim the old land of America in the name of the Narodniki. In the name of Uchitel," shouted the rider.

Some seventy miles away, Nul lay still, eyes closed, locked into the mystery of his own passing.

Chapter Seven

R YAN AND J. B. D IX were poring over a hand-drawn map of the redoubt and stockpile done on six separate sheets of paper, each one showing two different levels. The complexity of the place was staggering. It had more than seventy miles of interconnecting corridors and passages, with stairs and elevators between levels. The gateway was down on the fourth level, with the only viable exit to the bleak outside six levels below that.

Though the group had done a great deal of exploring, there were still considerable areas left where no one had been able to go.

"There be dragons," said Doc Tanner, coming up behind Ryan and J.B. and pointing with a scrawny finger at a blank area on the map.

"Dragons. What the fuck are they?" asked Ryan, straightening up from the table.

"Fire-breathing mutie lizards is the best explanation that I can offer, sir."

Behind the old man, J.B. raised his eyes to the ceiling and shook his head. Since they'd been in the redoubt, Ryan had suspected more than once that

Doc's sanity was returning. But often his behavior wasn't very encouraging.

"You never been up here before, Doc?"

"Never that I recall. But I fear that some of my brain cells have somehow become displaced. I can no longer remember all I might."

"Got to go, Ryan," said J.B., walking briskly to the door. "See you, Doc."

The door hissed shut. Ryan folded the maps and tucked them into an inside pocket of his coat. "Fireblast! We've been here six days. Could stay here the rest of our lives if we wanted."

"But do you want?"

"Don't know. Good place."

"Is it really, my dear Mr. Cawdor? If I may be frank with you, I confess that I have my doubts."

"Why?"

Doc moved closer to Ryan, his boots creaking. He half smiled, showing his oddly perfect set of gleaming teeth. His voice was its usual deep, rich tone.

"This redoubt raises so many questions in my poor, fuddled mind. Why only three survivors after a hundred years? And such an odd trio. Quint, Rachel and the dumb child, Lori. He is the Keeper. That's a hereditary position, and such positions bestow power without responsibility."

"You know he doesn't read, Doc?"

"Yes." The stovepipe hat dipped forward as Doc stared down at the floor. "Where are the others? He knows how to keep this place functioning by ritual and by rote. That is all.''

"That's nothin'. Most of the Trader's men couldn't read or write. But if you showed them somethin', they could do it. It's the way War Wag One was run.''

Doc nodded. "And yet...so many closed doors, are there not, my dear young friend.''

"Yes. We've tried to spring 'em but they've got good sec locks on 'em. If we blow 'em, then Quint would hear it. What do you reckon's behind 'em?''

"More of the past? More of the future? Surely, precious little of the present. I do not know, Mr. Cawdor.''

"Mebbe we should find out. But I tell you, Doc...I'm blocked to the back teeth with this place. This afternoon I'm goin' to get out and see some sky.''

"There are muties aplenty.''

"I know, but I've got security,'' he said, patting his guns.

"Cawdor,'' mused Doc, laying a forefinger alongside his thin nose. "Why does that name produce a distant and tiny murmur of a muffled bell?''

Ryan stared at him with his good eye. Unconsciously his hand strayed up to the livid scar that ran down his chillingly pale blue right eye, then moved down to tug at his lip on the same side.

"What...some legend of a great and powerful baron out East, beyond the Blue Ridges. Twin sons and a dreadful feud that ended... How did it end, Mr. Cawdor?" Showing a sudden ferocious glint of intelligence, Doc's eyes were bright and piercing as a mewed hawk's. For the first time since he'd known Doc Tanner, Ryan realized that the old man had once been a grim force to reckon with.

"I don't know what the fuck you're talkin' about, Doc. Your legend doesn't mean a thing to me."

"If it doesn't have...doesn't have...? Upon my soul, but it's gone again. What were we talking about?"

"The gateways, whether you'd found any clue how to work the bastard things."

Doc shook his head. "I fear not. I have discussed the matter with Mr. Quint, who tells me that the Keeper never knew about the gateway. Said that Special Ops MT ran them. I asked him what that meant and he didn't have any idea at all. The man is simply a gibbering parrot with no brain of his own."

"So we have a choice—stay here in Alaska, try and find transport back to Deathlands or risk the gateway again."

"Man gives birth astride a grave, Mr. Cawdor. What choice is that?"

Doc turned on his heel and quickly walked out, heading back toward their quarters. Ryan watched him, then decided that some food might be a good idea. He knew that eventually he had to get outside, away from the concrete walls and strip lights or risk losing part of his own sanity.

"YUMMY, YUMMY, it's the best for your tummy."

Finnegan threw the empty package on the table. The pizza it had contained was already cooking in one of the gray microwaves along the kitchen wall.

"Momma Maria says it's the best America makes," he continued, examining the bright wrapping, on which a stout, beaming, garishly made-up elderly woman held a skillet with a huge pizza on it while a brace of wide-eyed bambinos looked on hungrily.

Hunaker was waiting for her double beanburger to finish. "Free for fiber-fighters—Double discount vouchers at your local grocery," it said on the package, and in much smaller print, "Subject to availability. Offer closes June 1, 2001."

"By the time their offer closed, the whole world had closed as well," Hunaker observed.

All of them had taken advantage of the unbelievable range of clothes and supplies to dress and equip themselves better. But most of them had also kept some of their old gear. Doc kept his hat, frock coat and battered boots, but gave up his faded cream shirt for a new one in faded denim. Ryan kept his long coat, but took some new thermals, dark gray breeches, a brown shirt and a new pair of combat boots with high lacings to replace the old pair with a bite from a rabid mongrel on the right toe.

Finnegan and Hennings each picked similar outfits: high-necked jumpers in dark blue, with matching pants and black combat boots with steel toe caps. Okie kept her coveralls, choosing a sweater in light green for over the top. She also took a pair of low-heeled tan leather riding boots with the name Tony Lama inside.

Hunaker picked an exotic blouse in black satin with a pattern of leaves in green that matched her hair, gray cord trousers and gray ankle boots.

J.B. changed only his pants, which had been torn in a fight in the Darks. He searched the echoing hangar of the clothes store until he found a pair as nearly identical as possible.

Krysty found a new pair of coveralls, in her usual khaki. One problem they had was that clothes in unsealed or inadequately sealed boxes tended to fray and fall apart within hours of being worn. A pair of black leather trousers that Hennings had donned began to disintegrate almost instantly, resembling midnight lace within minutes after the air attacked them.

Krysty's one indulgence was in footwear. Lori went with her, tottering on her absurd high-heeled, thigh-length boots, the silver spurs jingling behind her. She took Krysty by the arm and led her to a section labeled Fashion & Working Boots—Top Names.

There they found row upon row of large white cardboard boxes arranged by size and by maker: Tex Robin, Dave Little, Henry Leopold, Larry Mahan and, the one she liked best, J. E. Turnipseede.

Miming her enthusiasm, Lori pulled down box after box, ripping out the contents of each to reveal a cascade of dazzling colors, and patterns and leathers. Lori rummaged through the piles, looking for one she thought Krysty might like. Her first choice had a heel nearly as high as her own boots, and Krysty waved them away, smiling and trying to make the mute girl understand that she would fall over in them.

"Those," she said, pointing to a pair in dark blue leather that had silver falcons with spread wings on the front. The tips of the pointed toes, finished in sharp, chiseled silver, seemed like lethal weapons. The heels were no higher than ordinary combat boots, and like the pair that Okie had chosen, Krysty's boots were made by someone called Tony Lama. As Krysty bent to try them on, her scarlet hair spread out in a brilliant wave over the dark calfskin of the boots. Then she stood up, feeling the snugness of the fit.

"They're just wonderful, Lori. Thanks a lot."

A shadow crossed the girl's face, as though someone had walked over her grave, but it vanished so quickly that Krysty wondered if she'd imagined it. But she knew that she hadn't.

"RIPENED IN THE SUN of Kansas and sweetened by the rain of Kansas," said Finnegan, tearing open a waxed pack of breakfast cereal. "What the fuck is Kansas?"

"It was a place, stupe," replied J. B. Dix. "In the east of Deathlands."

Ryan grinned. It was a little after noon and he was preparing to leave the redoubt. He'd hinted to the doddering Quint that he was thinking about it, and the old man had thrown a fit, spraying spittle as he gesticulated angrily.

"Keeper says not go. Those as goes is dead. Those as stays is the lucky ones. Don't try it. Many gone over the years, says the Keeper. Only us left. Lori got to have us a babe. Be next Keeper. Not Rachel, she's too fuckin' old for babes."

Cawdor hadn't argued with him. There was no point in rocking the boat. He and J.B. had discussed it and agreed that they should move on soon. In the redoubt the only thing you got was soft.

HUN, OKIE AND HENNINGS had become fascinated with some ancient vid and audio equipment they'd found in one of the cavernous stores. There were collections of films and TV programs as well as thousands of comp discs. Ryan had discovered similar stocks in other warehouses, but nothing on this massive scale. They could have played them for ten years and never have heard or seen the same thing twice.

Hun had taken a liking to a record called *Robert Zimmerman Meets Again with the Boys from the Band*. It seemed to be some sort of reunion concert from the year 2000, in some long-gone ville called Hibbing, Minnesota. She kept on playing it through a pocket quad with lightweight cans.

Okie watched endless programs on one of the TVs and was amazed by the amount of violence. A series based on a unit of sec men was her favorite and she bored the others with her enthusiasm.

"Listen, this little bastard called Belker is the greatest blaster you ever seen. Bites the shit out of the scum. But he don't kill as many as he should, probably to make him seem weak an' interestin'. He's got some real old guns—thirty-eights and Magnums." She turned suddenly and pointed at Ryan. "Do you feel lucky, punk?" she said, laughing hysterically.

Nobody else laughed. Nobody else understood what on the blasted earth she was laughing at.

Doc walked with Ryan down through the levels toward the exit. Not sharing an interest with the others in the old techno toys, Ryan contented himself with finding a library of crumbling paperback books—more than he had seen in his life, all gathered in one large room, with ladders to the high shelves and a balcony.

"Had you the time, my dear Ryan," said Doc, "then you would find the answer to every riddle known to man in this one library."

"The secret of who you are and how come you know so much about what happened before the Chill?"

"I like to speak to a man who likes to speak his mind. Indeed I do, sir. I would often tell Wilbur that."

"Wilbur? Who's Wilbur?"

Doc looked puzzled. "I have no recollection, I fear. Did I say Wilbur? Ah well... As to my past, Ryan, I fear it must remain locked away awhile longer."

"But one day, huh?"

"Perhaps, my dear Mr. Cawdor. Perhaps. Ah, here comes the delightful Miss Lori, teetering along so prettily. It is peculiar, don't you think, that she is so much younger than Quint and the harridan? An enigma shrouded in mystery, that."

The girl looked dazzlingly pretty to Ryan, her long golden hair tied back with a strand of emerald ribbon. Her red satin blouse had a small rip across the right breast, showing a tantalizing amount of flesh. Her short suede skirt clung tightly to her thighs, heightening her femininity. On her right hip was the holstered pearl-handled Walther PPK, apparently chambered for a .22 cartridge. Not much of a stopper unless you were very good with it.

"Hi," said Ryan, receiving a broad smile from the girl, and a nod.

"Leave you two young people together, I think," said Doc, grinning and bowing formally from the waist to Lori, walking off before Ryan could say anything.

"I'm goin' out," said Ryan.

Her head shook so violently that he feared she might have a fit.

"Yeah, want to see some outside. Seen enough inside for a while. You comin'?"

Again a shake of her head. She took his arm and tried to pull him back into the center of the redoubt.

"No, lady, I'm goin'. You stay. That's fine."

She kept her grip on his arm but made no further effort to check him. He walked along with her at his side, conscious of her attractiveness; wearing heels, she topped him by a couple of inches.

Ryan felt himself becoming aroused. Time was he'd have just laid her down in the passage and done it to her—without a single pang of conscience or regret. A woman asked for it with Ryan Cawdor, and a woman got it. Simple as icin' a stickie.

They descended the winding stairs level by level until they reached the tenth floor, which was near the bottom of the complex. At the base of the staircase, there was a pair of heavy steel doors, firmly locked. Ryan paused, wondering what the Keeper wanted to shut off in there.

"What's in there, Lori?"

Her face tightened with concentration. She put both hands to her cheek and closed her eyes, miming sleep.

"Beds? You come and sleep down here?"

Lori shook her head sadly. Then she bit her lip, trying again. She pointed to the doors and clutched her chest, rolled her eyes and sank slowly and gracefully to the floor, where she lay still, one leg bent beneath her. Not quite understanding the meaning of the pantomime, Ryan noticed that the girl wore no panties beneath the red suede skirt, and that her pubic hair was naturally as gold as her head.

"They...they're dead in there? Sleeping? Dead?"

She sat up with a radiant smile, then folded her arms around herself and shuddered.

"Frozen? Fireblast, you mean that there's folk in there, frozen and dead?"

She stood up, looking at him, mouth trembling open, almost as if she was about to talk. But the moment passed, and she turned and ran down a lateral corridor until all he heard was the tinkling of her spurs.

He stood for some seconds, looking at the great doors, wondering if the secret of the lost generations of the redoubt lay behind them. But whatever the secret was, he decided that it didn't much interest him. What he wanted was some fresh air.

He and J.B. had worked out the controls on a previous visit. The exit code was displayed on a green liquid panel. It was three digits. As soon as you pressed the Ready button, a return code appeared, three digits plus a letter to complete the sequence. Ryan touched the button that turned on the display panel. It showed 9.2.9. and the return code, 5.9.6. followed by the letter *H*.

The secondary entrance to the redoubt slid soundlessly open.

Ryan's nostrils were immediately filled with the stench of sulfur. Outside, sleet and snow whirled across a flat paved area about fifty paces square. In the stockpile they'd found dozens of snow buggies with tracks that enabled them to go over any kind of terrain. But for this brief excursion, Ryan had chosen to go on foot.

Repeating to himself, "Five, nine, six, *H*," he stepped through the door and watched it close behind him.

The landscape was as bleak as anything he'd ever seen. The redoubt was set into the side of a mountain. A long trail wound toward a steep valley below. There was no sign of vegetation anywhere.

He wore his thermals, with a thick sweater and his trusty long coat. The LAPA 5.56 mm was on his right hip, the steel panga on the left. The SIG-Sauer was holstered under the coat.

There were jagged peaks all around, vanishing into the murk, all of them layered with snow. The cold was intense, making him think that the rumors of the persisting nuclear winter were true. The sky was a sallow color, streaked like bile, showing occasional flashes of silver brightness from the chem debris that still permeated the heavens. Far off to the west, Ryan could make out a tall mountain with a smear of orange smoke trailing from it, indicating an active volcano.

For an instant, the ground vibrated beneath his feet from a minor earth tremor. Ryan steadied himself, rubbing his right eye to clear the irritation from the ocher clouds.

Squinting with his good eye, he spotted movement on the far side of the valley beneath an overhang of gray rock. It looked like a pair of huge bears, their coats of dirty white marked with yellow mud. As he watched them, they turned toward him.

Although the bears showed no sign of becoming a threat, Ryan drew the LAPA, holding it at the ready. They were probably a good half mile away as the mutie gulls flew, probably five miles by the shortest trail. Ironically, the two animals probably saved his life. Without them he wouldn't have drawn his gun.

The attackers came from above and behind. They dropped on top of Ryan and sent him crashing to the icy ground. He scrabbled to his feet, but just as he was upright again, one of them hit him behind the knees and he went flying to one side. But even as he fell, he snapped off a burst from his LAPA, the stream of lead stitching two of the five diminutive muties. They went spinning away, mouths open with screams, blood and intestines spilling from their torn stomachs.

As Ryan hit the ground, his gun struck rock with a solid cracking noise. His elbow and shoulder were jarred by the fall, but he was quickly up on one knee, steadying the gun at the three remaining dwarfs, who were shrouded in furs so that only their slit-eyes showed. One had obscenely long monkey arms that trailed in the snow as he moved. Another seemed to have a residual third leg sprouting from his left thigh. Ryan assumed that they were men, though there was no evidence either way. All three carried long spears tipped with barbed ivory points. Communicating with one another in grunts, they pointed at their two dying comrades and stamped their feet on the rocky ground in obvious rage.

"Come on, you little fuckers," said Ryan, holding his gun steady.

One of them waved his spear, shuffling nearer to the lone man. Still keeping them covered, Ryan slowly rose glancing around in case more muties were sneaking up behind him.

He held his fire as long as he could, though not out of any foolish milksop ideas of mercy or kindness. It was always good to know as much as possible about your enemies. Anyone not a friend was always an enemy. If Alaska was filled with these bloodthirsty muties, then it was as well to know what their weapons were. Did they have only spears?

They came closer, hissing menacingly, thrusting their wooden lances forward.

"Close enough," said Ryan, tightening his finger on the trigger.

There was a metallic grating sound, and nothing else happened. The fall had jammed the LAPA.

"Fireblast and shit!" snarled Ryan.

Chapter Eight

I hear that grim tyrant approaching,
That cruel and remorseless old foe,
And I lift up me glass in his honor,
Take a drink with bold Rosin the Beau.

The lyrics floated over the bare rocks, reaching the ears of the Russian guerrillas. The words made no sense at all to them. Had they understood them, they would still have been baffled, for the song came from distant antiquity. It dated centuries before the nukes fell from the skies, bringing the long darkness to all the world.

Zmeya came snaking back from the ridge, his clothes stained a dull green from the lichen that clung stubbornly to the lee of the boulders. He scurried to where Uchitel stood, holding his stallion quiet.

"One man alone, a trapper laying lines below the ice of a stream. Shall I kill him?"

"He is the first American. I would see him myself." Uchitel turned to the rest of the band. "Mount up, brothers and sisters. Let us to war."

The trapper, Jorgen Smith, was thirty-three years old and lived in a hamlet a few miles inland. His wife had been killed two years earlier by a pack of mutie wolves. They had had no children. Now he was content to venture out each morning—if the wind wasn't blowing to flay the skin off a man—and lay his traps for the beaver that still lived in the streams that ran fast and clean toward the sea. The water was saved from freezing only by the warm slopes of the live volcanos where the streams began.

Kneeling in the snow, he sang to himself as he worked, fighting the loneliness and isolation. His battered Remington M-700 sporting rifle was at his side in its sheath of caribou skin. The gun, a family heirloom, showed the scars of a hundred years of constant use. It fired 7 mm cartridges of which the community now had less than one hundred rounds left. Soon they would either have to barter for more, or rechamber the rifle. The Garand-type ejector—a spring-loaded plunger tucked in the bolt face—had broken in Jorgen's father's time, and a manual ejector had been rigged up by an itinerant blacksmith who visited each hamlet in the far northwest every two or three years.

"Remember me to one who lives there, for once she was a true love of mine," he sang.

Tying thin strips of rawhide, Smith fumbled with a stubborn knot, considering risking the removal of his gloves. He'd already lost his thumb and two fingers from his left hand by getting them wet and frozen the day he'd tried to rescue Jenny from the wolves.

He caught a glimmer of movement out of the corner of his eye where his goggles were cracked. Quickly pushing them up on his forehead, Jorgen reached for his rifle, dropping the trapping lines in the snow.

On the ridge behind him, silhouetted against the pallid sky, there was a man on a horse: a huge black stallion, much bigger than the little ponies that most folks ride. A gun of a design that Jorgen Smith could not identify, was slung across the man's shoulders.

The stranger was joined by a second rider, then a third and fourth, then more than Jorgen could count.

Holding his Remington, he stood up, waiting as they approached. To see so many strangers was something utterly beyond his experience. They could only be traders, with their goods on the pack horses at the rear of the column. But with their guns, they looked very threatening. Perhaps they were worried about muties. Guns were what kept muties away from the scattered villages.

Uchitel halted his stallion a dozen steps from the man, staring at him curiously, disappointed in a strange way that this American looked so like the wretched peasants on the Russian side of the Bering Strait. He wore torn and ragged furs, and boots that seemed to be no more than strips of cloth and leather wrapped around his feet.

"Hi, there," called Smith. "You tradin'? I've got some skins."

"What does he say, Uchitel? Should I kill him?"

"No, Pechal. Wait. I have a book that teaches how to talk to these Americans. It is here." Fumbling in his saddlebag, he pulled out a dog-eared volume.

On the front cover it said: "Convenient conversations for the the traveler for any eventuality." It was written by G. Duluoz and offered "Easy translations from the Russian tongue to the American and vice versa in seventy different social causes, with full index." It was published by Strafford Books in 1925.

Trying to be casual, Jorgen hooked his rifle so that it lay cradled in his arms, pointing in the general direction of the tall man with the kindly smile and the odd-colored eyes. Something was real wrong.

"You want directions somewhere? Are you lost? Where you from?" His finger touched the Remington's slim trigger, a three-inch nail that had been used to replace the original trigger when it had rusted through.

Uchitel ignored him, flicking through the pages until he found what he wanted. Holding the book in his right hand, he raised his voice so that the rest of the Narodniki could hear and admire. As he was about to begin, he heard a snigger.

"Perhaps, Krisa, I shall give you some cause for laughter in a while. You can laugh as your rat's belly is slit and filled with pyrotabs, then set on fire."

"I am sorry, Uchitel," whispered Krisa, blinking his narrow little red eyes in sudden gut-twisting fear.

"Who the fuck are you guys?" asked Jorgen Smith. "I don't know none of you."

To Uchitel, the man's accent was barbaric and grating, yet Uchitel still tried to communicate. "Good morning. Can you direct me us them to the house or mansion? We are awaited."

Jorgen's eyes opened wide with bewilderment. "What the fuck are you talkin' 'bout? You a fuckin' crowd of stupe muties?"

Uchitel tried again. He could feel a pulse beating at the corner of his right eye, which meant he was at risk of losing his temper. This imbecile was trying to make him look like a fool in front of everyone.

"We are—" he paused, deciding to use the Russian name "—Narodniki." He turned the pages with clumsy haste, his eyes brightening as he found what he wanted. "I he she it we they want wants food."

"Food! You crook-talkin' bastards want our food?"

Something was going wrong. Uchitel could sense it. He blinked, trying to clear the reddish mist that clouded his vision. The man facing them was waving his rifle in a way that was clearly threatening. They could all see that.

Stena, nicknamed the Wall because he was six feet tall and five feet wide, heeled his horse forward to the side of Uchitel. "The dog threatens us. Let me kill him, Uchitel?"

"*Nyet*. Wait."

"Get the fuck out, you snowsuckin' bastards! Go piss up an ice rope."

Jorgen put the Remington to his shoulder and aimed at the man who'd been doing the talking. Stena saw the move and kicked his heels into the flanks of his big bay mare and, yelping his delight, drew the 9 mm Makarov pistol from his belt.

Jorgen Smith's old gun barked first, the 7 mm bullet hitting the big Russian in the right shoulder. Stena fell from his saddle, landing with a great crash on his back in the snow.

Jorgen grinned at his success, frantically struggling with the makeshift manual ejector on the ancient Remington. A few yards away, Uchitel stood in the stirrups and yelled a command to his band.

"Do not shoot! *Nyet!* He is mine."

During his foraging through the ruins of Yakutsk, Uchitel had found a glass case among the rubble of some public building. A card had said that the item within the case had been used by "Comrade General Denisov in his valiant fight against the forces of capitalism and fascism during the first months of 1919."

Now it hung from the pommel of Uchitel's saddle, a long cavalry sword with a slightly curved blade, angled and weighted for a downward thrust from horseback. The hilt was padded with rotting maroon velvet tied with fine gold wire that had long frayed through. The ferrule was brass, the guard and knuckle bow, silver. An indentation on the back of the flat blade was engraved with hunting scenes. From the tip to the dog-head pommel, the sword was only two inches short of four feet.

As Jorgen prepared another round, Uchitel drew the saber from its leather sheath, feeling the cold hilt against his palm. Hearing the stamping of hooves, the American looked up at the last moment and parried the lethal down cut of the glittering sword with his rifle. Uchitel put so much force into the blow that it smashed clean through the stock of the rifle a couple of inches behind the finger guard, cutting Smith in the right shoulder. He dropped the splintered remains of the Remington, clapping his left hand to the bleeding wound.

"You done me, you bastard," he yelped plaintively, standing still and feeling his doom approach.

Uchitel swung the saber again. It sliced through the fur hood, skin, flesh and muscle, through the cervical vertebrae of Jorgen's neck, clean out the other side. For a long second, the corpse stood upright, head balanced precariously in place. Then the head rolled and toppled, bouncing on the stones to the cheers of the Narodniki. Blood gushed high in the cold air, the body slumping slowly to its knees, then folding on its side and lying still.

Uchitel wiped the blade of the saber on a handful of his stallion's mane, sheathing the sword once more.

"So die all who oppose the Narodniki," he called, pleased with his triumph.

"Not a bullet wasted," said Barkhat in his soft, gentle voice.

"One was wasted on me!" roared Stena, still holding his wounded shoulder.

"Is it bad, brother?" asked Uchitel. "Will you stay to seek poor Nul, wherever he might be?"

"No, brother, I ride on with you. Let us take more of these soft Americans."

"We shall take the entire land, brother," laughed Uchitel. He felt good. If this was the best this nation could do, then there was no need to fear.

Before they moved eastward, Uchitel carefully folded and put away the phrase book. It had been disappointing not to be able to use it more, but these peasants were such lackbrain weaklings that communication was hardly needed.

One last sentence caught his eye, and he spoke it carefully to the blood-sodden corpse, lying decapitated in the snow beside the gurgling brook.

"Much thanks for your help, sir," he said, trying to follow the phonetic pronunciation. "Here is a nickel for your trouble."

Uchitel heeled his black stallion eastward, and was followed by the others deeper into the bleakness of what had been Alaska.

Chapter Nine

RYAN PARRIED THE FIRST spear thrust, but cut his left hand on the white bone point. Grabbing the end of the shaft, he pulled hard, swinging the dwarf mutie to one side, knocking the second attacker off balance. With odds of three to one, he knew that he had to do something fast. The longer it went, the shorter his odds became.

He dropped the useless, jammed gun and tried to draw the steel machete from its sheath, but the muties were too close for that. And if he tried to go for the SIG-Sauer beneath his coat, they'd take him for sure. He had to buy himself a little time and space.

Holding the barbed end of the spear, Ryan screamed mightily and launched himself toward the creature holding the other end of the spear. The mutie slipped on the ice and nearly fell, loosening his hold on the spear. Ryan tried to wrench it from his grasp, but the gloved fingers clawed on to it. The muties had been expecting Ryan to keep away from them, and had been taken by surprise, but now the other two closed in again.

"Bastard!" spat Ryan, dodging a thrust aimed at his ribs from the mutie on the left, then moved a few steps toward the top of the track.

Knowing that the only way to fight close combat was bare-handed, he dropped his gloves. The hilt of the panga slipped into his fingers and he drew the blade, waving it in front of him in a singing curtain of death.

"Come on, now," he invited, waving the three muties toward him with his bleeding left hand.

Making little grunts and whistles, they seemed to be speaking to each other. Their slit eyes flicking nervously to him and then back, they spread into a half-circle about fifteen feet away from him. Above all, Ryan didn't want any of them sneaking behind him. Best defense was a good offense, he decided.

They had the advantage of reach with the long spears. If he let them keep him away, they'd kill him in the end, no doubt about that. Ryan watched them, noticing that the mutie to the left seemed crippled and moved slower and more clumsily than the other two.

He feinted to the right, making them back away from the whirling steel. Immediately he darted low and fast to the left, feeling the clunk of the blade cutting into flesh and bone. He'd hit the mutie just above the knee, parrying a spear thrust with his left hand. The little fur-clad figure toppled sideways, dropping its spear to the ice. The others hesitated, seeing their comrade down and done for.

Ryan didn't hesitate at all.

He slashed at the mutie's exposed shoulder and neck with the panga and simultaneously retrieved the wooden spear with his free hand. Blood jetted and the creature screamed, the furs falling back from its face. Ryan winced at the horror of the mutations in the dwarf's skull. It was squashed vertically so that the forehead rested squarely on the buried eyes. The distance between brows and chin couldn't have been more than three inches. There was also evidence of an appalling skin disease that had left the face raw and weeping, with crusts of small pustules nesting around the eyes, nose and mouth.

All of that registered in a splinter of frozen time as the machete descended, nearly beheading the mutie in a single blow.

Ryan turned away from the twitching corpse. He tossed the spear in the air, catching it in his right hand, and transferred the bloodied blade to his left.

The two surviving muties seemed torn between aggression and flight. Ryan solved the dilemma for them.

Reaching behind him like an athlete throwing a javelin, he hurled the clumsy spear with all his power at the nearest of the attackers. The sharp ivory point pierced the sealskin belt that the mutie wore about its sagging midriff, emerging with shreds of crimson flesh and gristle, slightly to the left of the spine. The creature lurched back, squeaking in a tiny, feeble voice, like a mouse with a broken leg.

Ryan saw that the mutie was done for. It had fallen on its side and was rolling back and forth, the long shaft of the spear scraping against ice and stones. Even in death, the mutie's gloved hands were clasped around the wood.

The last mutie—the one with the third, residual leg—was backing away, reaching under his furs with his left hand. Ryan watched him carefully, suspecting some kind of blaster. But all he pulled out was a tiny whistle of bone.

Before he could raise it to his lips, bringing who knows how many reinforcements, Ryan hurled himself toward the little figure. The gleaming ivory tip of the spear darted at him, but he parried with a ferocious cut of the panga, snapping the spear in half, the point falling to the ice and skittering away.

The mutie raised his hands to try to save himself from the death cut, but Ryan wasn't going to postpone the execution. Bone crunched as the steel blade smashed through the mutie's fur-clad right wrist, severing the hand so that it dropped like a furry animal. Blood gushed out, warm and salty, into Ryan's face, nearly blinding him. But he quickly wiped his eye clear, cutting again at the blurred figure before him.

The machete penetrated the mutie's shoulder almost to the breast. Ryan pushed at the creature's face, knocking him down. Putting a boot on its throat, he jerked the blood-slick metal clear, then jammed it through the fur hood where he guessed the mouth should be. He heard teeth splinter and felt the shock run clear up his arm as the tip of the panga penetrated through the back of the mutie's neck into the frozen earth.

For a moment he left it there, the thonged hilt sodden with fresh blood. He straightened up, looking around to make sure no more muties were around the entrance to the redoubt. The wind still howled and snow flurries obscured the view. He suddenly remembered the two monstrous white bears that he'd seen a few minutes ago and decided that it might be safer inside.

He pulled the panga clear of the dead mutie's skull, wiped it on the creature's fur jacket, and slipped it back into its sheath. He saw the LAPA lying on the stones, a dusting of snow already building up around it. With a shrug he left it there and turned back to the door, punching in the return code of 5.9.6., then the *H*.

Nothing happened for a breath-stopping moment, then the vanadium steel swung open and Ryan returned to the warmth and security of the redoubt.

Back in their living quarters, the first person he saw was J.B. The Armorer looked impassively at

Ryan's torn and blood-soaked clothes and came as close as he ever did to a smile.

"Fresh air good, Ryan?" he asked.

"I've had better," Ryan replied.

PREDICTABLY, IT WAS J. B. DIX who discovered the museum of arms and armaments.

"I can smell guns," he said. "Followed the scent of oil and steel and lead and grease and brass. Found it up on top level. Even got ob slits. See for miles."

"See what?" Ryan asked.

"Nothin'. Snow. Couple of volcanoes north and east. Sky full of chem clouds and general nuke shit. Lot of yellow, from the smokies, I guess. Come an' see it."

Ryan grunted in reply, but didn't move, continuing to eat in silence, oblivious to the rest of the group. Something peculiar was happening in the redoubt. Three of the microwaves had already stopped working. Several of the sealed clothes stores that Quint had allowed them to open were showing signs of rapid deterioration, with garments becoming frayed and actually rotting. The water-purifying plant in their dormitory had started to malfunction, sometimes providing a thin green scummy liquid that smelled of death. Ryan had talked about this with J.B. only the night before, and they'd agreed that the redoubt and stockpile had been sealed against outsiders for so many years that their presence had upset the delicate balance of the machinery. Quint was obviously aware of it and kept asking them when they were going to leave. Yet, oddly, some of them got the feeling that he didn't want them to go.

They finished their evening meal, chucking the disposable plates and cutlery down the garbage chute. Finn paused by the sliding panel for a moment, listening.

"Fuckin' funny noises down there. Like rocks grindin' against each other."

With J.B. leading the way, they left the dining room and headed for the armaments museum, marking their progress on their own maps. From ingrained caution, they paused at every turn of the corridor. They saw no sign of Quint, Rachel or Lori as they advanced quietly up to the top of the stockpile.

"Here," J.B. said, putting his hand against an illuminated rectangle set flush in the wall to the right of a door. The door slid silently open, revealing a foyer. On the wall there was a sign.

"Do not touch exhibits. Ammo filed beneath under cross-refs," read Krysty.

"Look there," said Ryan, pointing to another sign, hand painted, not neatly printed like the other one.

It's nice to come, if you've got your pass.
But if you don't we'll bust your ass.

The double doors at the far side of the foyer had small circles of glass set in their tops. Ryan pushed them open, stopping so suddenly that Hennings walked into him.

"Fireblast!"

"What the . . . Oh, fuckin' . . ."

The museum stretched out ahead of them, dim lights brightening in the large hall as sensors detected their presence. It wasn't the array of weapons that caught everyone's eyes. It was what was nailed to the floor just in front of them.

All of them recognized it as the mummified corpse of a young child. Either it had been assembled by a crazed and skilful surgeon, or it was one of the worst mutations that any of them had ever seen. Despite the dried, leathery skin, it was possible to make out scars from what had once been suppurating sores all over the body. The umbilical cord dangled like a knotted brown string, and a shrunken penis revealed the original sex of the child. Though it looked to be only a few weeks old, it had a full set of needle-sharp teeth, and its fingernails were long and curved like claws. Ryan counted nine fingers on the right hand. The left hand sprouted from near the shoulder. It looked like a little paddle of lacy skin and had at least a dozen fingers on it. The legs were less than three inches in length, ending in toes that lacked nails.

At the shoulders there were the stubs of what looked like the wings of a prehistoric flying reptile. The crucified baby had two heads, one with only a residual stump of a skull, hardly visible in the shadows. The ribs were appallingly distorted, running more from top to bottom than from side to side, and the pelvis was strangely tilted, obscenely large for the rest of the torso.

A long thin dagger with a hilt of twisted silver wire was pushed through the crossed feet. A second blade pinned the right hand. A third was pressed through the scrawny throat. Blood darkened the tiles all around the body. Hunaker touched it with the toe of her new tan boots, watching it crumble to powder.

"Been here for years. Mebbe twenty or more. Could be plenty more."

There was a message that had apparently been scrawled with a finger, using blood that was still warm and fresh. The words misspelled and the letters clumsy, it was difficult to read, but clearly a warning:

"Kep oute for evver ore dy." It was signed, "The Keper."

"You said Quint couldn't read or write," Ryan said to Krysty.

"Yeah. No reason to lie, was there?"

Ryan shook his head. "Guess not. So, if he's as fuckin' old as he looks, an' he's the Keeper . . . who was the Keeper who wrote this?"

J.B. pushed past him. "Who cares, friend? Let's go look at some guns."

And what guns they were.

Some of them were at least three hundred years old, looking frail and dusty inside cases of Plexiglas. The party split up to wander around, and the huge room echoed with their cries of amazement at the wonders. Ryan walked with Krysty and J.B.

It wasn't just a boggling array of blasters. There were all kinds of daggers and swords and axes. Many of the guns had descriptive cards under them. One card read, "Pair English flintlock night pistols, circa 1712, made in England by James Freeman. Screwbarrel guns fired buckshot instead of conventional ball, making it easier to hit a target at night, hence their name."

"What kind of range would that have, J.B.?" asked Ryan.

"I guess about twenty feet on a good day, or night," replied the Armorer, and moved on to explore on his own.

In the next case was a delicate sword with a blade that tapered to a needle point. Krysty put her arm on Ryan's, squeezing against him. "When do we go, lover?" she asked.

"Soon. Mebbe tomorrow. Day after for sure. Sword like that wouldn't be worth mutie shit in a firefight."

The card read, "English small sword, officer's. Circa 1765, steel hilt, with colichemarde blade. Grip bound in silver wire. Pierced pommel and guard. Blade length, thirty-two inches."

"Look at the length of this mother, J.B.," yelled Okie, her face pressed against a case across the hall. The long dark hair in her ponytail swung back and forth with her excitement. Dix joined her, reading slowly from the card.

"Model eighteen-forty-two rifle-musket. Fired the seven-forty grain Minie ball. Sights up to...up to nine hundred yards."

"Over a fuckin' half mile," gasped Okie. "That right, J.B.?"

"I'd back it up to about eighty yards."

"Look at the barrel on it," said Ryan, joining them. "Must be over five feet long."

"Couldn't get that inside your coat," grinned Krysty.

"Wouldn't want to."

"You goin' to change that LAPA now?" asked J.B. "On through there, under that arch, is an armory of modern stuff. Get somethin' new."

"What?"

J.B.'s sallow face warmed with a smile, and his eyes twinkled behind the thick lenses of his glasses. "Go see. I saw somethin' you might like."

Ryan walked quickly away, hearing the click of Krysty's dark blue cowboy boots following. He slowed down and waited for her, passing Finnegan and Hennings, immaculate in their matching blue jumpers.

"How's the hand, Ryan?" asked the fat man.

He inspected it. A little dried blood was crusted around the cut from the mutie's spear tip, but it looked clean. Ryan knew that out east there were villages of "dirties" who lived in mud huts and used poison on their arrows. The Trader had told him about them.

"Better, thanks, Finn."

On either side, rows of cases were stacked one above the other. He knew that J. B. Dix had a few precious booklets and pages torn from mags that showed some blasters from before the Chill. Now those blasters were in front of him and he read the names on the cards.

"Colt. Remington. Walker. Sharps, Smith & Wesson, Winchester, Le Mat, Luger, Gatling, Maxim, Walther, Browning, Kalashnikov, Thompson, Mannlicher, Schmeisser, Uzi, Mauser, Tokarev, Webley, Deringer and Deringer, Tranter." His voice faded in wonder at this staggering array of arms. "J.B. could stay here all his days, Krysty. This is what his life is all about. Blasters in all shapes and sizes. Look at 'em. Just look."

He never even noticed the tiny vid camera hidden in the shadows near the ceiling, its tiny lens darting from side to side, following the movements of the group.

Just as they'd raided the clothes stores, so everyone took their pickings from the section of the museum beyond the arch, where there were rows and rows of greased and oiled blasters in all sizes and shapes and calibers; grenades and bombs and mines and rockets; bayonets and gren launchers; strangling wires and bazookas; machine guns and poison pistols.

Hunaker replaced the broad-bladed dagger that she'd broken fighting the Sioux in the Darks; barely a week earlier, it seemed like a dozen lifetimes. On J.B.'s recommendation, she took a 9 mm Ingram submachine gun that pared everything down to the minimum. Despite its small size, the light bolt action gave it a staggering rate of fire close to fifteen hundred rounds per minute. The card said it was the model 12. She also took a supply of the stick mags.

Okie kept her M-16A1 carbine with the collapsed stock, adding to it an IMI Mini-Uzi submachine gun. It weighed just over six pounds and was less than fifteen inches in length.

Krysty liked the clean, silvered finish on a Heckler & Koch P-7A 13 pistol, which fired a 9 mm bullet out of a thirteen-round magazine. Because of the large number of rounds it held, there was a special insulating block in front of the trigger to absorb heat from the gas that retarded the slide opening. J.B. nodded his approval of her choice.

Finnegan and Hennings both went for the fifteen-round model 92 Beretta pistol with frame-mounted safety, firing a 9 mm round.

They both liked a whole rack of dull gray Heckler & Koch submachine guns with built-in silencers and fifty-round drum magazines; they fired single, triple or continuous bursts of 9 mm bullets. The card said it was a development of the famous HK-54A2 model of the 1990s.

Ryan watched J.B., strolling around the rooms of new guns, hands behind his back, lips moving as though he was silently praying. But he wasn't. He was simply comparing the various qualities of the blasters ranged all around him.

"Can't do much better than what I've got," he finally said, watching the others carry armfuls of ammo down to their dormitory.

He pulled out his Steyr AUG 5.6 mm. "Nice Browning Hi-Power over there. Might take a Mini-Uzi like Okie got. Useful if we meet a mess of muties. And a new knife or two. Mebbe stock up on grens, huh?"

There was a polite cough from behind. The men spun, each dropping instinctively into a fighter's crouch.

"My apologies, gentlemen, if I caused a shimmer of nervousness to trickle through your bodies."

"Just fuck off, Doc," said J.B., relaxing, pushing back the brim of his crumpled fedora, fumbling in his pocket for one of his favored cheroots.

"I have taken the liberty of arming myself, if you have no objection, so I can be less of a weight for you to bear on our little jaunts."

"Jaunts?" exclaimed Ryan. "What kind a blasters you got?"

"An uncle of mine, a dear, sweet man, once owned a handgun of some rarity. A weapon for the connoisseur. Also, in the right hands, one to blast off the balls of a demented stickie, if I may be excused a lapse into the vernacular."

"You may, Doc. You fuckin' may," said Ryan, smiling.

"I have taken this to aid me in my striding over the difficult terrain we seem to encounter."

He held a long ebony walking stick in his right hand. As he tossed it in the air and caught it, the glittering silver pommel was revealed. It was a beautiful carving of the head of some ferocious animal with great teeth and a mane of hair.

"Handsome, Doc," said J.B. admiringly.

"More than that, my dear Mr. Dix. *Voilà!*" With a twist of the hand he loosened the head, drawing out a snaking rapier of polished steel from within the ebony shell. "From the plant of elegance, I pluck the flower of mortality."

"What about a blaster, Doc? Nice sword, though."

"Grudging praise from you, Mr. Dix, is better than the most fulsome flattery from the lips of lesser mortals. Yes, as I said, I believe..." He paused, looking confused. "Did I mention the handgun that an uncle...?"

"Yeah," said Ryan. "Go on."

"I saw it. Here it is." He pulled a massive blaster from the front of his frock coat.

"It's a double-barrel cannon, Doc!" exclaimed J.B. "Le Mat, ain't it? Heard of 'em. Never thought I'd see one."

Ryan extended a hand for the pistol, nearly dropping it, surprised by the weight. Doc Tanner also handed him the card that had been in the showcase.

It read, "A nine-chambered percussion revolver designed by Dr. Jean Alexandre François Le Mat of New Orleans in 1856, being granted U.S. Patent 15925. Manufactured in Louisiana by Pierre Beauregard, later to fight as General for the Confederate States Army at Manassas and Shiloh. This model of a .36 caliber. The unusual element of a Le Mat pistol is that it also has a second, central, smooth-bore barrel, to take a .63-caliber scattergun round. The nose of the hammer is manually adjustable."

"Big muzzle, looks about eighteen bore," said J. B. Dix, holding the heavy blaster. "Could be good. Got ammo for it, Doc?"

"Ample, Mr. Dix, thank you. I shall take it down to our quarters. Are we to try the gateway or do we go for the great outdoors?"

"You haven't found nothin' to help operate that fireblasted gateway, Doc?" asked Ryan.

"Only what I knew already."

There it was again, the peculiar suggestion that Doc Tanner had somehow been around these redoubts before the Chill. Which was clearly impossible. That was a hundred years ago. Doc might be a muddled old fool most of the time, but he wasn't *that* old. You could lay an ace on the line about that.

"So how do you know that, Doc?" asked Ryan, seeing the same question on J.B.'s lips.

"I'm not too—" He stopped speaking, looking up beyond Ryan's head into the dark shadows that clung to the corners of the high room beyond one of the narrow ob slits. "There is a vid camera up there, moving to watch us. I fear that the Keeper will know we have intruded into his sanctum sanctorum."

"His what?" asked J.B., his face creasing with irritation.

"Guess Doc means we've pissed in Quint's best pot," said Ryan. "We should go."

"Doc, you go. Take as much ammo as you can carry. Tell the others to keep to the dorm. Ryan, come with me. Somethin' you've got to see."

Doc holstered his Le Mat and shuffled off, the tip of his sword stick rapping on the floor. Ryan followed J.B. through a smaller arch into yet another gallery of weapons.

There it was, complete with ammo of all sorts, including rounds of tracer. And a thin booklet giving a full account of the gun and how to strip and service it.

"In the big fire," said Ryan, whistling his surprise. "That's for me! What about the others?"

"No time," replied J.B. "They got what they got. You take this. I'll carry as much ammo as I can. Let's go."

It was a rectangle of metal with a night scope on the top and a pistol-grip butt and trigger on the bottom and was unlike any other weapon that Ryan had ever seen. The name was on the side, just below the sight. Heckler & Koch, Model G-12 recoilless rifle.

The outside of the book gave the main facts, and they were amazing. It fired single shot like any ordinary rifle. On continuous fire it worked at six hundred rounds per minute. But in three-shot bursts it fired at over two thousand rounds a minute: a staggering rate. The other innovation was that the 4.7 mm cartridges were caseless, which meant that he could carry a much greater supply of ammo than with a conventional weapon.

Flicking through the manual, Ryan's eye was caught by several facts he wanted to study at greater leisure. But right now, with the vids recording his every move, it would be smart to leave. He snatched the gun—nearly dropping it because of the film of oil that still covered it—filled his coat pockets with mixed ammo and quickly followed the disappearing figure of J. B. Dix.

"THE BIG HUNK CALLED JOE just gotten himself iced," said Okie through a mouthful of doughnut. She was watching yet another old police serial, *Hill Street Blues*.

Ryan was lying on his narrow bed, perusing the arms manual for his new gun, occasionally helping himself from a bag of mutlicolored sugary sweets called *Jelly beans* that Krysty had found.

Finn and Hennings were playing a noisy vid game called "Klingon Blasters." Hun was stretched out on her bed, running her fingers through her green hair, listening to some music called *soul* on her cans.

Doc was lying on his own bed, eyes closed, chest moving regularly in sleep. J.B. was muttering to himself as he tried to persuade one of the microwaves to disgorge several cheese-filled portions of chicken breast.

"I'm the Klingon expert, you stupe," yelped Finn, excitedly.

Henn walked away disgustedly. "Fuckin' Klingons. Next time we'll play for creds."

"What'll you spend it on?" asked Krysty, sitting by Ryan, brushing her long, flaming hair, allowing it to spread in fiery waves across her shoulders.

"A fifty-shot mag on this beauty, J.B.," called Ryan, cradling his new toy.

"Doesn't tumble like the five-fifty-six does. Won't mebbe do the damage, but I figure it's better for— well, look who we got here."

Everyone turned, except Hun, who was deafened by her own music. Standing at the door was the Keeper, paying them a visit.

Quint was flanked by his two wives, Rachel grinning toothlessly on his left, Lori a couple of paces behind on the right. All three of them were holding their MP-5 SD-2 silenced submachine guns under their arms, in a casual, unthreatening way.

Ryan immediately began to feel concern. Not one of them actually had easy access to a loaded blaster. Indeed, Hun, eyes closed, humming away to herself, still hadn't seen them.

His deep-set eyes were rheumy, red-rimmed and his straggly beard was stained with some sort of sticky oil, but Quint was nodding and smiling. He stopped about twenty paces from them.

"Keeper says greetings to our guests. First guests in a long day. Savin' those as sleeps down below. Sleeps the long sleep as ordered by the Keeper, don't they, my dear?" he asked Rachel, who nodded like a child's doll.

"Glad you've come, Keeper Quint," said Ryan, standing by his bed, signaling behind his back with his fingers, warning the others that he didn't like the course things were taking—warning them to be as ready as they could without actually taking any provocative action.

"The Keeper comes and goes when he wishes. When are you goin'?" he snapped, the colored ribbons fluttering in his beard.

"Day after tomorrow," replied Ryan.

"Eh?"

"He said they're goin' day after next, Quint," said Rachel.

"Keeper says mebbe. Mebbe they will and mebbe they won't."

Ryan Cawdor's eye was caught by the young girl, Lori. Standing just behind the old man, her husband, her mouth kept opening and closing, as though she was about to faint. In the quiet, Ryan heard her spurs tinkling.

"We go when we please, old man," J.B. said.

"Don't you speak to my brother like that, you glass-eyed shitter!" spat Rachel.

"Brother!" exclaimed Finnegan. "Thought he was your husband."

"Ah, you clever fat prick, he is. Brother. Husband. I'm his wife."

"Then . . . ?" said Ryan, pointing to Lori.

"Oh, the dummy. She's his daughter's daughter. Don't have the brains of a frozen piss hole."

For a few moments everyone was silent, trying to assess the situation. Hun broke the stillness by get-

ting up from her bed, starting to dance to the music.
But she suddenly saw Quint and the others in their
frozen tableau.

"What the fuck does...?" She pulled off the
earphones, and they could all hear the shrill, tinny
music.

"Keeper says you been wicked. Keeper says you
been to see the place where death lives."

His voice was becoming louder and more queru-
lous, with spittle spraying from his lips, dangling in
his beard. Ryan noticed that the knuckles of the old
man's right hand were whitening on the trigger of the
Heckler & Koch. The sequins on his jacket shim-
mered in the overhead lights.

"Keeper says the law is set on them as breaks it.
Keeper's word runs like the law of maintenance. To
venture without is to die. To break..."

There was no warning.

Lori suddenly moved, pushing past Quint, sending him staggering into Rachel, running toward
Ryan, dropping her own gun. Mouth open. Talking.

Screaming!

"It's trap! They kill! Kill 'em, Ryan!"

The room exploded with violence.

Chapter Ten

BRITVA HAD AMPUTATED three toes from his right foot, using the open cutthroat razor that had given him his nickname. After his fall into a pool a few days earlier it hadn't been possible to stop and light a pyrotab to dry out his socks and boots—not without running the risk of being abandoned as the unlamented Nul had been. So he'd waited and hoped. But eventually the blackness had come and the swelling. The toes had bled very little.

Uchitel had watched him closely for any sign of weakness, but the little man with the trimmed beard had kept up well.

The invasion was going better than he'd hoped. The one disappointment was that Alaska was just as poor as Russia.

The two communities they'd found and destroyed so far were even smaller than those across the ice river. One had consisted of only three wretched hovels containing seven human beings, four of them with strong mutie traits. Three of the locals had killed themselves as soon as they saw the invaders looming out of the driven snow.

But one of them had been kept alive: a lad of around eighteen in surprisingly good health, despite being riddled with lice.

Uchitel prodded his stallion to move faster. The temperature was dropping fast as night approached, and shelter was yet another couple of miles away, in the lee of a low ridge. Since arriving in America, Uchitel no longer felt the need to keep checking behind him. Those horseback soldiers, if they really did exist, would have given up days back, not daring to leave their own terrain.

The American boy had given them hope of better days to come.

Pechal had taken the lad, helped by Urach, watched carefully by Uchitel, who had held his phrase book open on his lap. The boy was stripped and tied to a skinning frame outside the hut where his mother lay raped, sodomized and dead.

After his failure with the trapper, the leader of the Narodniki had spent time studying the book, gradually learning how to choose his words with greater care. Now, he felt ready.

"Where are big house and store?" he asked, trying to pronounce each word the way the book said.

"What?"

Pechal laid a thumb on the boy's right eye and pressed; the boy screamed and tensed his skinny white body against the cords. Blood trickled from his burst nails, and his ribs stood out like a line of picket fencing. The pain was so severe that the boy lost control of both bladder and bowels simultaneously, making Pechal curse and step hastily away from him.

"Don't hurt him, Pechal. Not yet. I have read how America was a place of great riches. Everyone owned several houses and trucks and guns. It cannot be far to such places. I will ask him again."

Bizabraznia, the Ugly One, came swaggering by, clutching an earthenware beaker of *zubrovka*. From her walk, it was obvious she had drunk several mugs of the spirit already. She looked at the naked boy, reaching out and grabbing him by the genitals.

"If he won't fucking talk, Uchitel, then I'll fucking rip off his fucking balls. Hear him sing then."

"Leave him be."

All three of Uchitel's followers looked at him, hearing the familiar crack of command. The woman staggered unsteadily off toward the others, who were cooking a stew of root vegetables. Urach backed away from the helpless boy, resheathing one of his surgical-steel knives. Pechal pulled the gray hood of his long cloak over his head, bowing slightly. But Uchitel noticed how Sorrow's long curved nails were driven so hard against the palms of his hands that crescents of blood showed brightly.

"We would like to visit some reputable stores. Which do you recommend?" asked Uchitel, moving closer to the helpless youth, careful to avoid the fouled snow.

"Stores, mister?" gasped the boy. "I heard tell of 'em. Where Traders go. Ain't none. Not for a month's march there ain't."

Though most of the boy's words were incomprehensible to Uchitel, the negativity was clear. There was a long silence while he thumbed through the book.

"Can you direct me to the best place to buy a real bargain, if you please? Thank you."

"I don't know nothin' 'bout nothin', mister. Swear to the blessed savior, Jesus Christ crucified, I know fuckin' nothin'. I can't help you."

Uchitel blinked, fighting to control his temper. His translation book wasn't getting him anywhere. At the last hamlet he made the mistake of speaking to an old man only to find the dotard was deaf as granite. It had been a mercy to slit his throat for him. But now he was still failing. Failing was something that Uchitel didn't like.

"I will try again. I think his head is filled with ice," he said to the other two.

The boy stared from one to the other, his face twitching with nerves, the cold making his whole body tremble. Already the yellow snow around his bare feet was turning to ice. These barbarians with such awesome blasters had come from the west. But everyone knew there was nothing to the west, just a land where chaos ruled and muties lived. The gross woman who had tugged at his penis with her rough hands had been frightening, but the one who was their leader and who was trying to speak to him in a crooked and halting tongue was the worst.

He had eyes of gold, like the ferocious mutie wolves that ravaged the land and were hunted for their furs. Never had the boy seen a man with such eyes. The face was kindly, the mouth full lipped and generous. Yet the young lad could hardly breathe for the fear the man inspired.

If only he knew what the man wanted, he would tell him. Tell him anything. If his family hadn't already been butchered, the lad would betray them now for his own life.

"I request you direct me to where I can find food and clothes."

It was Uchitel's last try. If this didn't work.

Suddenly an idea came to the boy. They wanted to find some place where there were clothes and food in abundance.

"Yes," he said.

"Da?" queried Uchitel.

"I know what you want. I heard tell of it. Ain't here. Ain't never seen it. Don't know anyone who has, but I heard tell of—" The boy stopped as Uchitel waved a warning hand, frantically turned pages of his tattered little book and finally found what he wanted. "Slowly, if you please, madam. I am a stranger and a visitor to your land."

"Slowly? Sure. You want the stoppile. Word is it's filled with stuff like you want. But my Dad said it was all bear shit. Doesn't exist. Anyways, folks go there and they die there. That's what they say."

"Stoppile?" repeated Uchitel. "Clothes and food?"

"Sure, mister. Stoppile. Near where Ank Ridge used to be."

Uchitel shook his head. "Where?" he asked, smiling to himself at the obvious wonderment he could read on the faces of Urach and Pechal.

"Near Ank Ridge. That way," he said, gesturing with his head to the southeast.

Uchitel tweaked the lad's cheek, much as a kindly uncle would after his favorite nephew had answered some arcane riddle.

"He tells me that there is a place of great wealth southeast of here, called stoppile, near a place called Ank Ridge." Uchitel consulted the book again to make sure he'd understood the boy. "Yes, the boy is right. Tell the others we will go at dawn."

"And what of him?"

"The boy?"

"Da," replied Pechal in his gentle voice. "What of him?"

"Kill him." It was a matter of supreme indifference to Uchitel now.

The boy died in appalling agony at the hands of Pyeka, the Baker, their incendiary expert. Pyeka found a novel way of introducing elongated pyro-tabs into the youth's body, then lighting them. Pyeka had always thrived on the laughter and praise of his comrades for his cleverness with fire.

The next morning, having forgotten the threat of the cavalry at his back, Uchitel led his group toward Stoppile near Ank Ridge.

South and east toward the stockpile not far from where Anchorage had once stood.

Chapter Eleven

LEAD STREAMED OUT of the silenced MP-5 SD-2s
held by Quint and Rachel. The silenced Heckler &
Koch blasters fired subsonic rounds, with little more
noise than a man coughing. But their effect was
devastating in the long, forty-bed dormitory.

When Lori made her move, screaming out a
warning, the room became a bedlam of noise and
movement. For an instant, Ryan was frozen by the
cry from a girl everyone had thought totally dumb.
Then he dived for cover, hitting the floor and crawling toward his bed and weaponry; knowing, as he
did, that he was likely to be too slow.

He glimpsed feet. They were scrabbling and running everywhere. As he rose, squinting around the
bottom of his bed, he took in at a glance what was
happening.

Quint and Rachel still stood near the doorway,
firing their blasters from the hip. Quint was cackling with maniacal laughter, and Rachel's face was
frozen in a rictus of savage hatred. Bullets skittered
off the wall, striking sparks from the row of lockers.

"Ice 'em!" J. B. Dix shouted from across the room.

"Talk's fuckin' cheap," muttered Ryan, trying to reach the hem of his long coat; he wanted to drag it from his bed and get at the SIG-Sauer P-226. Another burst of fire exploded along the floor, only inches from his outstretched hand, making him retreat. Then he had the coat and then the pistol, knowing immediately from its weight that it held the full complement of fifteen 9-mm rounds in the mag.

As he maneuvered into position for a clear shot, he heard a piercing scream and saw Lori fall in a tangle of flying red clothes, crimson smearing her face.

"Fireblast!" he cursed, seeing that Quint had moved behind the lockers, only the heavy muzzle of the submachine gun protruding. Rachel had also taken cover behind a bed, cackling her delight at having shot her own great-niece.

He could see only a couple of his own group. Finnegan was crawling toward his bed, after his new model 92 Beretta, hanging in its holster from the bedframe.

And Hunaker.

Her cropped green stubble of hair gleamed in the overhead lights. Hun was marvelously athletic, with exceptional strength and agility. Her own Ingram 9 mm was on the floor, resting against the television. Ryan's eye was caught for a moment by the picture on the screen of a naked couple in bed—a thin-faced man and a beautiful woman with long dark hair.

Making her move, Hun dived into a forward roll, then reached for the blaster. She was straightening when Rachel saw her. The crone hobbled a step sideways, screeched a warning to her husband-brother, then opened up with a burst of continuous fire that ripped into the crouching girl.

Hunaker was hit across the chest, the bullets unzipping her clothes and skin and flesh. She was thrown sideways onto her back. The gun fell from her fingers. She tried to get up again but fell forward in a crouch, her head between her knees, coughing up blood.

"Fuckin' bastard!" screamed Okie, moving toward the dying woman.

"Get back!" ordered Ryan, seeing that Okie would be cold meat for Rachel. But the harridan was too busy laughing at her success. She shouted to Quint, "Done the green bitch, Keeper! Done the..."

Ryan held the stamped steel pistol in his right hand, steadying his aim with his left. Engraved along the top of the barrel in tiny italic script were the words, *Schweizerische Industrie-Gesellschaft,* J.P. Sauer & Sohn, Eckenforde.

He aligned the leaf front sight with the vee of the back, centering it on the crowing old woman. He squeezed the trigger three times in rapid succession.

Blood appeared among the tatters of leather that hung about Rachel's body. Her cap with its tawdry glass beads went flying from her matted gray hair, rattling in a corner of the room. Her arms flung out as though she was trying to stop a runaway horse, and she took three tottering steps backward. She sat on a bed behind her, then rolled onto her side and remained still.

Kicking on the floor, hands to her face, Lori was screaming on a single monotonous note that grated at the nerves. J.B. and Hennings had both got hold of their guns and were opening up on Quint, keeping the malevolent old man cowering behind his makeshift metal barricade. Finnegan had also got hold of his blaster, and Okie had managed to reach her own bed, taking up the M-16A1 carbine.

There was no sign of Doc at all.

Hunaker was moaning only five paces from where Ryan crouched, his warm pistol in his hand, awaiting a chance to waste the Keeper. A lake of blood was spreading slowly from beneath the girl, seeping over the floor.

There was a momentary lull in the fighting. On the television, a kitten appeared for a moment, in a surreal flash from a century back. Hun's headphones still poured out the thin sound of a song about a dock on a bay.

"Ryan." Her voice was the faintest whisper.

"What is it?"

"I'm done, Ryan."

At least four bullets had hit her, dead center in her chest, and Ryan knew it. It would be absurd and dishonest to pretend she would be okay.

"Are you in pain?"

"Not bad. Numb. Mebbe I'll be gone 'fore it fuckin' starts."

"Could be."

Another burst of fire from the others ripped into the lockers and walls around Quint. There was no reply at all.

"Ryan, think you'll ever get to see Sukie again?" asked Hun.

It was a moment before he figured out who she was talking about. Then he remembered. Sukie was the pretty little girl who'd joined War Wag One from War Wag Three just before the shambles of Mocsin. He recalled that Hun had been paying some attention to her.

"If I see her, Hun, I'll tell her. Take it easy, now."

Hunaker was wearing her new black satin blouse with green leaves embroidered on it. The blood didn't show on it at all.

"Don't shoot no more. Keeper says to put up the blasters. Keeper says he'll yield."

Ryan Cawdor stayed where he was, shouting to the old man, "Gun first, Quint. Then you, hands high as you can get 'em."

Nothing happened for some seconds. Then: "Keeper says how can he trust you?"

"Do it. You have my word nobody'll ice you. But throw out the gun first."

There was a tiny sound from Hunaker, and Ryan looked back to where she was huddled.

"Hun? Hun, can you hear me?"

There was an unmistakable stillness to the green-headed girl, and Ryan knew she was gone.

Krysty was close behind him. "Dead?"

"Yeah."

"Don't like to think of her dyin' like that, kind of on her own."

Ryan looked around and saw there were tears glistening at the corners of the girl's eyes. "We all have to, you know."

"You swear you won't hurt Keeper? You done for poor, sweet Rachel and little Lori."

"That murderous old slut blasted the kid," shouted Henn.

"Didn't have to chill Rachel."

"Come out, old man," yelled Ryan, the pistol rock steady in his right fist.

"Swear I'm safe."

"You're safe, Quint. Come on, before we come and gun you out of there."

Now they were all standing, all pointing their blasters at where Quint was cowering. Even Doc had finally appeared, clutching the Le Mat cannon in both hands.

"Here's the gun," yelped Quint, tossing the Heckler & Koch on the floor. It skidded and bounced, finishing up a yard or two from Ryan's feet.

"Watch the bastard," warned J.B., who was right behind Ryan. "Could have a hider up his sleeve."

"Yeah. Watch him."

"Keeper's comin' out. Ally, ally oxen free. Don't shoot poor old Keeper. He had to do it. Rules is rules and the law's the fuckin' law, ain't it? You understand, don't ya?"

"Move it!" shouted Ryan, feeling his anger rising. He'd liked Hunaker. She'd been a friend for about three years.

"You promised the Keeper," mumbled Quint, cringing as he left his cover.

His sequinned jacket flashed, gaudy and cheap. The heel had broken on the woman's boot he wore, and he limped, his hands trembling in the air. A thread of spittle dangled from his thin lips, and he was shaking like an aspen in a hurricane.

"Promised Keeper," he repeated.

Ryan put a 9-mm bullet between the deep-set eyes, sending the old man crashing backward, arms flailing, mouth dropping open in shock.

Ryan holstered his pistol, not even bothering to watch the death throes of the last Keeper of the Anchorage Redoubt. A man didn't get up when he'd been rained on with a 9 mm through the forehead at twenty paces.

"Turn off the vid and Hun's music," he ordered. "Drag those two stiffs out of here. J.B.?"

"Yeah?"

"We'll move out tomorrow. First light. Get all the maps you can. Take Finn and Okie and get some buggies serviced and fueled up. Henn, you and Krysty take charge of stocks of food, pyrotabs, spare snospex, ammo, grens, thermals," he said, ticking off items on his fingers as they occurred to him.

"What may I do to be of service, Mr. Cawdor?" asked Doc, struggling to force the big pistol into its holster.

"Check the gateway's exit and entrance codes. Might come back here for another jump if there's nothing much around. Look out for muties about the stockpile."

"What about her?" asked Okie, pointing contemptuously to where Lori was weeping on the floor, holding bloodied fingers to her face. "Shall I ice her?"

"We'd all be iced if she hadn't shouted," suggested J.B. "How bad is she hurt?"

The girl sat up then, looking around at the angry, tense faces. "Got bullet across head from Keeper." She showed the wound, a livid crease on her head among the blond hair. The wound was clotted with blood that was already drying. It didn't look too bad.

"What should I do with the gateway, Mr. Cawdor?" asked Doc, oblivious of the fact that the conversation had moved on.

"Just look it over. Make sure there's nothin' wrong with it. You know more about them than we fuckin' do, Doc, don't you?"

The old man shook his head in bewilderment. "I fear that my memory is rather like a train, Mr. Cawdor. The farther it pulls away, the smaller it gets."

"What about her?" asked Finn. "She saved us, but she's kin to those dirty bastards."

"Take me," begged the girl. "Take Lori or Lori die here."

"Anybody else for wastin' her?" Ryan asked. Nobody replied. "We take her, then. Okie. Get her bandaged if she needs it."

"What about Hun?" asked the girl blaster.

"Can't bury her. Anyone seen any crems? Lori? Anyplace bodies can be burned or whatever?"

"I show you room where they put some."

"Sure. Doc, you can help. After Lori's cleaned up, go with her, and take Hun down to where she shows you. Some kind of freezin' place, I guess. Use one of the plug-in buggies around. Take those two—" he indicated the corpses of Rachel and Quint "—and dump them out the door near the freezin' place. Check the return code."

"Triple number followed by a letter was common in these places, as I recall," said Doc.

"Sure. Come on, people. Let's all get movin'."

SUPPER WAS A DOLEFUL MEAL. More of the microwaves had gone on the blink, and the long room stank of burned food. At least it helped to drown out the sour-sweet scent of death. Finn suggested that they move to another of the linked dormitories for the last night, but everyone felt too tired to bother.

Ryan and J.B. had agreed on what they'd do. The maps showed a large town called Anchorage on the coast. Seemed worth a careful recon to see what remained.

All the maps were loaded; also food, heating supplies, ammo and all the blasters they wanted. Lori's cut had been wiped and disinfected, and she was in good shape, talking excitedly about leaving the stockpile for the first time. Okie was the only one who made her dislike felt. The others simply accepted Lori as one of their own.

The buggies were juiced and ready to roll.

Doc had been unable to open the door to the chambers where they thought bodies might be frozen and stored, so the corpses of Hunaker, Quint and Rachel had been placed outside the door. "Won't hurt Hun now," Ryan had said. Doc had also carefully noted the current reentry code and each of them had it written down and memorized. It was the numbers one, zero, eight, followed by the letter *J*.

Each ice buggy held three or four people, with plenty of storage room for extra gas and supplies. Ryan was to drive the lead vehicle with Krysty; J.B. would take the second with Lori and Finnegan; Hennings would share the third with Okie and Doc.

The vehicles were already heavily armed with mortars and machine guns. Judging from his encounter with the local muties, Ryan figured they should be more than able to wipe out any opposition.

At the suggestion of J. B. Dix, everyone went to bed early that night to be ready for a dawn start.

Krysty came to Ryan, in the night, whispering that they should go to the next dormitory, where the beds were clean and the smell of death was missing, and where they could make love without being overheard.

They found a bed in the other dorm, and she held him tight, her long hair brushing against his shoulders. "How do you feel about Hun?" she asked.

"Like I lost my blaster," he replied.

"No feeling?"

He shook his head. "No. Hun was good. But she got iced. Maybe you tomorrow, me the next day. Start feelin' sorry and it doesn't never stop."

"Doesn't *ever* stop," she corrected him, feeling a tremor from his chest as he laughed at her.

"Sure."

"If it had been me?"

He leaned over her, his single eye glittering in the dim light. "You're different, Krysty. You know that."

"You're sort of special, too."

Before dawn they fell asleep, tangled in each other's arms, having made love three times.

AFTER THEY'D DRIVEN the buggies onto the small gale-swept plateau beside the redoubt, they gathered for a last word from Ryan.

"We've got radios, so let's keep in touch. We're Buggy One. J.B.'s Two and Henn's Three. Use the radio only if you have to. Should be able to keep in visual touch. J.B.'s got the maps. We're heading toward where the town of Anchorage was. Should get close by evening."

As he spoke, the ground trembled under their feet and some powdery snow came cascading from the cliff above the redoubt's entrance. "Only a little quake," said J.B. "Plenty of those mothers where you've got volcanoes. Taste the sulfur on your tongue."

The gale was gathering force, and Doc nearly lost his tall stovepipe hat; he secured it with an elastic beneath his chin. "This hurricane puts me in mind of a jest I was once told," he said, half-shouting to be heard above the wind.

"A jest? You mean a joke?" asked Krysty. "I recall Peter Maritza back in Harmony using that word for somethin' funny. Said it was a word his grandfather used and he kind of remembered it."

Doc nodded, wiping a tear from the corner of his eye. "This damned wind! It appears that many, many years ago, back in Kansas, there was a herd of longhorn cattle."

"Was longhorns some sort of muties?" asked Finnegan, curiously.

"Not really, young man. They were grazing out on the open grasslands when a dreadful gale arose. A positive typhoon, it was. And it began to blow ever more strongly toward these cattle."

"Get to the fuckin' point, Doc. I'm freezin' my fuckin' tits off," moaned Okie, huddling against the chill.

"My apologies, madam, though I hardly feel that my style of discourse merits such foul language from such pretty lips. I will proceed. The wind eventually blew with such ferocity that the entire group of cows were lifted from their feet and whisked away over the horizon. They became known forever after as the herd shot round the world."

It was obviously the punchline, so everyone laughed appreciatively. As they climbed into their buggies, Krysty tugged at Ryan's sleeve. "You get that joke of Doc's, lover?"

He grinned at her. "No. Couldn't understand it."

Once everyone was aboard, they set off toward the city of Anchorage.

Chapter Twelve

THE NARODNIKI WERE on the right road. They knew that because the mutie woman had told them before they used and abused her, finally spilling her tripe in the snow with the curved blade of the bayonet of a Kalashnikov.

"Ank Ridge?" had been the question from Uchitel. "Stoppile and Ank Ridge."

She'd responded to the latter name, gesturing to the south. Her mouth was so misshapen, with only a residual tongue, that she could do no more than nod and point.

So they moved on: a long line of people, heavily furred against the bitter nuclear winter, heeling their ponies and horses toward the rising sun, rifles slung across shoulders, food and ammo weighing down the pack animals. Their eyes were cold as ice, and many of them wore clothes splattered with dried blood.

So far they had seen no signs of the legendary dangers that had for so long prevented anyone from the Russian side crossing the frozen strait. There had been no sign of flaming hot spots or of giant muties fifty feet tall with eyes of fire and claws of steel. Nor was the land utterly barren. Here and there were patches of earth free of snow, pocked and dappled with dark green mosses and stubbly grass.

They had met little opposition to their plans to drive inland. Apart from the loss of Nul, and Stena's unfortunate shoulder wound, there had been few casualties on this trip, and they had lost only two men, both to a single rifleman a day back. The sniper had ridden on a slope overlooking the hamlet they were ravaging and had shot down both men from cover. Then, as the angry guerrillas charged him, he had put a bullet through his own skull.

Two dead, three if he counted the absent Nul, Uchitel thought. Only one injured, two if he allowed for the three toes that Britva had self-amputated.

Their journey to Stoppile was taking much longer than Uchitel had been led to expect. After a two-week southeasterly trek across the Alaskan interior, they'd encountered an impossible mountain range. Changing their course to the northeast, they'd eventually found a trail that led south through the mountains. Unknown to the Narodniki, they were traveling along the earthquake-riven remains of what had once been the main highway linking Anchorage and Fairbanks.

Now that they were finally drawing close to Ank Ridge and Stoppile, Uchitel was well pleased with himself, and as they rode along, he sang an old, old ballad about the stars being the sentinels for mankind. He liked the verse about the importance of order over chaos. It appealed to his sense of the rightness of things.

Far off to the left he glimpsed the skulking shapes of a pack of mutie wolves, their bellies flat to the tundra, shadowing the party. They must be disappointed, thought Uchitel, that there were no weak stragglers in his band as there might be in a herd of caribou—stragglers that they could drag down and rend apart.

There were no weak stragglers in the Narodniki.

Toward evening the ground shook with one of the worst quakes since they'd crossed into Alaska. Rocks on a slope of ice-bound boulders ahead of them broke free and cascaded down noisily, nearly blocking the trail. The horses were frightened, and several riders, including the massive Bizabraznia, were unseated. Angered by the mocking laughter, she grabbed her animal's bridle and delivered a fearsome punch to the horse's head, knocking it to its knees. Then she kicked and lashed it with her whip until it returned to its feet. As she remounted, she was rewarded with cheers from her fellows.

Uchitel touched the cold hilt of his saber, remembering the good feeling of decapitating an enemy. He wanted to capture more enemies so that he could use the sword once more. Perhaps in the town of Ank Ridge there would be plenty of chances.

When the wind shifted to the south he caught the bitter taste of salt on his tongue, in addition to the ever-present sulfur from the surrounding volcanoes. The salt meant the sea could not be far away, which meant that Ank Ridge must also be close.

Grom, their explosives expert, reined in his horse alongside Uchitel. "That would make a fine show for my toys," he shouted. Grom was almost stone deaf and shouted all the time.

Grom pointed to a large dam with towers, set across a valley to their left. It dominated the valley where they rode, silhouetted against the amber sky, which was splashed with streaks of vivid green lightning.

"The water will be frozen, Grom," he called, facing him so Grom could read his lips.

"No, Uchitel! See ahead, there is a river that flows and there is green to its sides. Away beyond that dam you see the smoking cone of a volcano. It heats the water so that it flows. Let me burst it and wash all away down here. It would be a fine sight, I swear."

"Not now, brother. Perhaps another day, but not yet. Not now!"

"WHAT IS THAT, UCHITEL?"

Evening was dragging its murky cloak across the wasteland, the yellow clouds turning a sullen maroon. It had snowed a little during the late part of the afternoon, dusting the trail ahead. The dam was still visible behind them. This time it was Barkhat, with the smooth, velvet voice, who spoke; as he did so, the puckered scar at the corner of his mouth twitched and danced.

"Where?"

"Yonder. Like a large ball."

Uchitel strained his eyes into the gloom. He saw several squat buildings and a large saucer-shaped object, which was cracked along one side and mounted on a tripod. It was difficult to judge its size, but it looked to be about a hundred feet in height. There was also a huge ball, half as high again, that seemed to be made from a complicated pattern of interwoven triangles. Uchitel had never seen anything like it, but it nagged at his memory. There had been something like it in one of the old history books in Yakutsk.

"I think it was a defense against firefights."

"What?"

Uchitel nodded, the facts trickling back into his mind. "It was called *radar*, Barkhat. It was a way of seeing great distances and watching for enemies. There were many such installations along the coasts. I have read that such buildings stood where the Sakhalin and Kamchatka lands were. But they were—" he hesitated, seeking the expression that he'd read "—*Da,* they were 'primary objectives' for the nukes. This one must have been missed."

"Should we go look, Uchitel? Might there not be much gold?"

"Imbecile! Would there be gold after a hundred years? They were not places of wealth. No. Let us ride on by."

"Perhaps we could camp there if the buildings are safe."

Uchitel considered it. "Perhaps, brother. Perhaps we can."

"And watch for enemies," added Urach, who'd come in time to hear the latter part of the conversation.

"Our enemies are all ahead of us. We need no radar to tell us that."

"None behind?" asked Urach.

"*Nyet,*" replied Uchitel, forcefully. "If there were, then they stayed back in Russia. They will never be a threat to the Narodniki."

ONE HUNDRED AND FIFTY MILES behind the Narodniki, Major Gregori Zimyanin was leading his group of one hundred mounted militia. They were at the foothills of the Alaskan Range, spread well out, the horses picking their way carefully through the torturous mountain terrain.

Aliev, the Tracker, was a little ahead of them, waving them forward. Zimyanin had deliberately held up the crossing of the Bering Strait, hesitant at the enormousness of what he was doing, and uncertain whether the party would approve.

But now that he was closing in on his prey, some three or four days behind, it was time to press forward at all speed. As his horse crested a rise, the officer's heart filled with pride.

This might be just the beginning.

Chapter Thirteen

THE CRUCIFIX WAS BLACKENED and seared by the fires from the heavens. Icicles hung in the crevices around the twisted, tortured form nailed to the metal cross. The fingers were gone, so were the tips of the thorned crown, melted away a century back. The flesh of the crucified Christ was satin black, like the wing of a crow, polished by the ceaseless wind to a velvet consistency.

It stood bolted firmly to the tottering remnants of what had once been the side of a small brick church almost under the haunting shadow of a mountain. Its twenty-thousand-foot summit was permanently obscured by snow spume and chem clouds.

Around the crucifix, kneeling on the sharp stones, were about twenty people, most of them women. They wore dark clothes wrapped around them in layers, giving them a funereal appearance. Their leader, a tall skeletal figure with wild eyes and long black hair, was standing in front of them, facing the crucifix.

"Blessed are the nukes," he called.

His congregation responded, "And blessed shall be the fallout."

"Blessed is the punishment of the Dark Lord."

"And blessed are the nails of his hands and his feet."

"Blessed are the long chill and the many rads."

"Blessed be both the short heat and the long cold," came the response.

"We wait thy coming, Lord."

"Aye, we await thy black visage."

"Then shall we be released from bondage and into eternal life among those in the bunkers below."

The man turned then to gaze out at them. "In this place, tainted by the blood of many, shall we stay until He cometh to lead us to salvation. Amen, amen, amen."

"Amen," pattered the others, rising one by one.

At that moment they heard the distant sound of engines, throbbing and whining off to the south.

ANCHORAGE WAS GONE.

They stopped the three buggies and got out on a bluff overlooking the sullen expanse of gray-green ocean. J.B. and Ryan checked their maps, glancing at the compass for bearings. There wasn't any doubt.

What had once been a sizable city had totally disappeared.

"Nukes," said J.B. tersely, his sallow face showing no emotion.

"Yeah," agreed Ryan Cawdor. "Nukes. Must have wasted all round here, hot-spotted it, triggering quakes, or mebbe volcanoes. That's a big crater out there." He pointed to the east, where a smudge of smoke showed against the pale sky.

"Crater," said Doc Tanner. "Why should that ring a distant bell? I fear me I do not remember."

"Quakes dropped the cliffs in the sea. Up came the sea, and there Anchorage went."

The wind was so strong that it was blowing a waterfall that flowed over the cliffs back into a rainbow arch over their heads, drenching them. It wasn't a place to hang around, with some particularly vicious gulls gathering and swooping.

"You could throw out those fuckin' maps," said Okie. "The whole fuckin' place is changed."

"Mebbe not away from the coast. There's another big town shown, Fairbanks. We'll make for that."

After only six or seven miles of uneven driving, Ryan slowed, waiting for the others to come alongside. Not bothering with the radio, he stuck his head through a side ob slit and shouted, "Somethin' ahead. See 'em?"

In a shallow valley almost on the flanks of the high mountain was a huddle of buildings. Some of them looked desolate and ruined. Among the buildings stood a small group of about a dozen people, shrouded in dark clothing.

"They seen us," shouted Hennings, his black face almost invisible within the wrappings of clothing he wore against the bitter cold.

"Fingers on triggers," warned J.B. "Remember the Keeper. Let's go."

Oddly, none of the waiting group moved as the buggies came grinding closer, kicking up a spray of snow and ice behind them. In each buggy someone in the top bubble was manning the light machine gun, covering the strangers. At a signal from Ryan, the vehicles stopped about thirty paces from the watchers.

An extremely tall man, his face exposed to the elements, strode toward them, his hand raised in the universal sign of peace.

Ryan noticed the dark crucifix on the wall behind the man, recognizing it as a symbol of the old religion. Over years of traveling with the Trader they'd come across a few ruined churches, but they'd never been of any interest and obviously held nothing of real value, like food or blasters.

"Cut the engines down to idle," he ordered, using the radio. "These people don't look dangerous—they're mainly women, and I can't see anyone in the huts—but keep alert."

"Welcome," called the emaciated man. "Welcome in the name of the Dark Lord."

"Is that a baron?" asked Krysty. Ryan shook his head.

"If you come in peace, we will share with you what little we have. As we are all gathered here at the river by the throne of our Lord, we welcome you. Step down from your wagons."

Ryan flicked the switch on the speaker. "You got blasters?"

"Weapons are an abomination against our beliefs. We carry clean steel and that is all."

Ryan looked at Krysty, who shrugged. "I don't know, lover. We need some local knowledge. Do you think mebbe they can help?"

He nodded. "I'm goin' out. If there's no trouble, then you come. Tell J.B. and his team to follow, then Henn and his team last of all. All right?"

"Sure."

Ryan opened the hydraulic door, stepping out on the snow, holding his new G-12 caseless automatic rifle casually at the ready. "My name is Ryan Cawdor," he said. "These are my friends." The sweep of his arm took in the buggies and their occupants.

"My name is Apostle Ezekiel Herne, and these are the sisters and brothers of the Church of the Dark Lord Waiting. We have dwelled here in this field of blood for many years now, coming together from all over Laska."

Ryan looked around, beckoning Krysty to follow him. The sight of the tall girl with her tumbling mane of brilliant red hair brought chattering from the women. Their talk was quelled by an angry glare from their skinny priest.

"This is Krysty Wroth," he said. Then, as the occupants of the second buggy emerged, he continued, "The guy in the battered hat there is J. B. Dix, and the fat man's Finnegan. The lady with hair like straw is called Lori."

"What is straw, Brother Cawdor?" asked Herne.

"Let us pass, friend," replied Ryan, waving to the occupants of the third buggy to come out. They followed his lead, all of them hefting blasters ostentatiously, ready for action.

"The old-timer is called Doctor Theophilus Tanner, and the lady's name is Okie."

The black man was last out, holding his gray Heckler & Koch 54A submachine gun with its built-in silencer. As he stepped down he threw off his thermal hood, showing his face and his mass of cropped, curly hair.

The effect of Hennings's appearance was amazing. Everyone except for Herne gave a great cry of terror and exultation and fell immediately to their knees, prostrating themselves on the barren stones, moaning and shouting. Ryan and his party dropped into defensive positions, fingers tight on triggers, eyes flicking nervously. A single wrong move, and all of Herne's group would be iced.

The priest himself stood still, trembling and shaking, hands clutched together in front of him, his long bony fingers tangling like a nest of worms. His voice shook when he finally spoke.

"Lord, Lord, you have come. As it was foretold in the great books of defense and survival, you walk again among us."

"Lead us to salvation, Dark Lord," screamed one of the women, scrabbling forward on hands and knees toward the black man, who nervously backed away from her. But she seized him by the ankles and pressed her chapped lips to the steel toe cap of one of his polished black combat boots. Licking the gleaming leather, she writhed in ecstasy.

"Get this fuckin' gaudy slut away from me, Ryan," said Hennings, raising his blaster as if to crack it into the woman's skull.

"Oh, Lord," called Herne. "It is said that a man such as you would one day come to us. All our prayers and teachin' is for that."

"What does he mean, a man like me?" asked Henn.

The priest answered, pointing to the nuke-blackened Christ upon the tumbled wall. "There is our tortured messiah. Never in our lives has such a man been seen."

"I knew it, Henn," cackled Finn.

"What, stupe?"

"One day it'd be good news havin' a black man ridin' as my shotgun. Now it's come. These sons of bitches fuckin' worship you, Henn."

"IT'S TRUE, J.B.," said Ryan, as they ate the last of the turnip stew and meat. None of them knew what the meat was, and nobody wanted to ask.

"Henn a god, just 'cos he's black. I don't believe it, Ryan."

Ezekiel Herne had led them to the largest hut, and had ordered two women to feed them and arrange their bedding. Ryan had made sure that the three buggies were locked and that small contact mines were placed and primed. He also made sure that the community knew it, so no one would tamper with the vehicles.

Hennings had been taken into another room and fed on his own. He'd protested strongly until Ryan pointed out that these people were ready to worship him, and if that meant free food and some guidance around the country, then being a god for a few hours wasn't such a bad thing.

After they'd eaten, the cadaverous priest came to them, sat crosslegged on the floor beside Ryan and grinned at him with the worst set of rotten teeth that Ryan had ever seen.

"You have brought such happiness to us here, my friend. You are blessed to be the brothers and sisters of the Dark Lord. Is there anything we can do for you?"

"Sure," said J.B. "Tell us, what happened to Anchorage? And tell us also, are there any sizable towns round here?"

Herne's brow furrowed. "Towns are the abomination of the blessed, my friend. Ank Ridge, as we call it, was the Sodom of this barren desert. The seas rose and those monsters that dwell in the deeps came and washed away all evil. There are no towns left in all the world, friend. It is better so."

"No other villes? No small villages?"

"Nothin', my friend. There is the snow and the ice, both good things. A wind upon the mount. Who would wish to die, my friend? Not while the Dark Lord is here."

"What do you think Henn is goin' to do for you?" asked Okie.

"Henn, as you call him, is the chosen one, the awaited one, the one whose comin' will make all right. As the books say, the sheaves shall be harvested and bound, the chaff shall be winnowed, the blood shall give life."

"Blood, Reverend?" asked Doc quickly. "What blood?"

Herne stood up, knee joints cracking. "All will be seen, friends, tomorrow at dawn, when we gather to worship him as he shall be ordained."

"Is Henn goin' to be sleepin' in here?" asked Finn.

"No." Herne's gentle smile sent shivers up Ryan's spine. "The sisters wish the honor of fucking the Dark Lord. He will sleep little, as the plow sleeps not in the furrow."

Okie sniffed and spat, then went to one of the low truckle beds and sat down. The priest watched her, then moved to the door.

"We shall see you all on the morrow. One of the sisters will bring in a bowl of punch for you to drink your fill. It will aid you at sleeping."

He left, banging the heavy door shut behind him. Finn giggled. "That lucky son of a bitch bastard, Henn. Gettin' all that for free."

A great crock of drink was brought in and set on a table by one of the younger women. She was wrapped in black cloth from head to toe, and her face was veiled so that only her brown eyes shone from under the cowl. Finn tried to get her to talk, but she lowered her head and ignored him, leaving quickly.

"Can't wait to get back to her Dark Lord," Finn said, ruefully.

They tried the punch. Ryan wrinkled his mouth at the taste. It was flavored with herbs and obviously was strongly alcoholic. But as he rolled it cautiously around his mouth, he detected a strange, bitter aftertaste. He spat it out on the earthen floor.

"Fireblast! That's evil stuff."

J.B. put his mug down on the table. "Don't care for it. Tastes like wolfbane."

Lori had taken more than a bit of it before her face showed her dislike. "Not like," she said.

"Seems drinkable," belched Finnegan. "Bit of ... yeah, not so good."

Okie, Krysty and Doc put down their beakers, untasted. Ryan looked across at J.B. biting his lip, knowing that the Armorer shared his doubts. But neither of them said anything. After all their years together, they didn't need to.

Ryan tipped the bowl in a dark corner of the room. The punch flowed into the dirt and left only a faint damp patch. When Herne returned, he seemed pleased to find that the punch was gone.

"I shall leave you now to sleep. Our celebrations begin at dawn. I doubt they will disturb you."

TOWARD MIDNIGHT Finnegan fell asleep, snoring loudly. J.B. checked him, the light of the dying fire reflecting redly off his glasses. "Seems well out. Can't wake him easily. Heart's all right. Breathin's deep but steady. Best take turns to watch him."

The hut shook as a momentary earthquake vibrated across the land. Tremors had become so common that nobody even noticed them.

They quickly arranged a roster to sleep so that one of them would always be awake, checking that Finn wasn't ill. Ryan guessed Finn couldn't have drunk enough of the punch to do him any permanent harm. But the mere idea of it was enough to make them more cautious overall. Okie agreed to sleep across the doorway, and all of them kept their blasters ready and primed. J.B. suggested breaking out, there and then, taking Henn with them, but Ryan was for patience.

"The food was fine and it doesn't seem dangerous here. Plus we're warm. It might not have been a sleeper in the drink—could be just strong liquor. Finn hasn't had any for weeks now. We'll watch 'em."

RYAN CAWDOR AND KRYSTY WROTH were now accepted by the others as a couple. They went together, drove together and slept together. Once in the redoubt, Okie had made a play for Ryan in front of Krysty, putting her hand directly on the front of his trousers, smiling at his instant reaction, glancing at Krysty.

"Looks like he's ready for a fuckin' change," she had said.

Ryan had tensed, ready to deck her with a roundhouse right, pulling himself away from her grasp.

Krysty moved toward Okie, smiling at her with even white teeth. "Ever try anythin' like that again, slut, and I'll put two holes through the back of your head."

Ryan had rarely heard such menace in a human voice. Okie backed off, her eyes flicking nervously from Krysty to Ryan. "Only a joke, Krysty. Can't you take a fuckin' joke?"

"Yeah. See me laughin'? Make sure, Okie, you know the difference between a threat and a promise. Then you'll know what that was."

Okie never tried it again.

Now Krysty and Ryan were pressed together in a single bed, like spoons in a box. She faced away from him, her hair brushing against his chest, making his nipples feel tender. He almost immediately became erect, but both of them were sleeping fully dressed, even down to their boots. But she could still feel his need for her.

"Have to be a quickie, lover," she whispered.

"Better than nothin'. Want a hand?"

"No. You handle your part and I'll do the rest."

While he unzipped his trousers, she wriggled out of hers, pulling them down to her knees. She kept her panties on, moving them to one side to accommodate him. He felt the warmth of her muscular buttocks cupping him and he slid easily into her warm waiting depths. She moaned softly at the size that slowly filled her. He moved in faster and deeper, keeping the rhythm even so that she could share his pleasure.

"Yes, lover," Krysty whispered. "Keep it for... yeah, that's good. Hold me tight."

As he came, Ryan threw his head back, arching his spine so that he could thrust against her as hard as possible. The girl moaned again, and he could feel her internal muscles fluttering and tightening as she reached her own driving climax.

They slept until near dawn, when J.B. came and shook Ryan by the shoulder.

"What?"

"Turn out. It's close to first light. Your duty now. I've seen nothin' and heard nothin'."

Ryan swung out of bed, hastily doing up his trousers.

"One other thing, Ryan," said J.B.

"What's that?"

"Sometime last night they locked the door on us, bolted it on the outside. Oh, and Finn's out colder than an iced mutie. But I figure he's goin' to pull through. His pulse is still regular and steady. I'll stay awake."

"Mebbe wake everyone else," suggested Ryan, standing up and stretching like a great cat.

"Yeah," agreed J.B.

Silently they got ready, leaving their chubby companion snoring quietly on his bed, his mouth sagging open. As they checked their weapons, Ryan saw that Lori was looking terrified.

"Don't worry," he said. "Just takin' care."

She nodded to him, her lips trembling.

Attractive though her gear had been, Ryan had insisted that Lori change before they'd left the redoubt. The tall blonde now wore dark green combat coveralls tucked into steel-capped boots of the type that Finnegan and Hennings wore. She'd kept her little pearl-handled Walther PPK .22 pistol and also the Heckler & Koch MP-5 SD-2 silenced submachine gun that she'd toted around the stockpile.

"All ready?" he asked.

"Someone movin' out there," said Krysty, her ear pressed against the locked door. "Several people."

Ryan, who had known Krysty long enough to trust her amazingly acute hearing, moved to stand by her and saw the dawn's faint light around the edges of the door. There was also a crack of light near the center panel, where the thick wood had split. He put his eye to the crack but couldn't make out anything. Quietly he drew his panga and probed at the gap with the long blade, widening the split a little.

He squinted through it with his right eye.

Someone was standing near the other side of the door, blocking the view. Then the person moved and Ryan blinked at the sudden brightness. The sun had broken through the heavy cloud, giving a rare vision of a full dawn. He saw a space of trampled earth and snow immediately in front of the building; the broken wall, with its sinister, fire-blackened crucifix, faced him.

In front of the wall a low platform had been contrived from old wooden boxes. Resembling a rough table, the platform was about six feet by four feet. Several women, all hooded, were ranged around it, along with their leader, Ezekiel Herne. The rest of the community stood nearby in a half-circle, hands folded into their long sleeves.

"What's goin' on?" asked J.B.

"Can't tell. Some sort of ritual. Worshipin' the dawn or—"

Herne's ringing voice stopped Ryan's words. His breath pluming in the bitter cold, the priest said, "Accept this our sacrifice . . . the greatest we can offer. Take our Dark Lord."

He lifted his hand: Ryan saw that it contained a broad-bladed dagger of glittering obsidian. The women around the table parted, and at last he could see the object of their attention.

Bound with black ropes, naked and seemingly unconscious, lay Hennings.

The knife began to descend.

Chapter Fourteen

"Noooooo!"

Ryan's yell of rage was probably the only thing that could have checked the falling blade.

There was no time to fire a gun to save Henn, no time to blast open the door and ice the crazed priest. But the shout made Herne hesitate, and the blade slid past Henn's naked chest.

"Krysty, quick!" said Ryan.

The girl didn't need encouragement. Ryan's response had been so electric that it meant instant action.

With long, slender fingers, she gripped the edge of the door where the frame was warped by the cold. Her eyes closed and her lips tightened. Through gritted teeth she whispered the incantation to enable her to draw on her hidden power.

"Mother, Earth Mother, help me. Help me... now!" The last word sounded as if it were torn from her heart.

Metal screeched and wood splintered and daylight burst into their room around the shattered door. Ryan was first out, followed immediately by Okie, then J.B., all of them opening fire on the murderous group.

Ryan's new G-12 was set on three-round bursts, giving him a lethal firing rate. The caseless bullets tore through the black-robed women standing around Hennings. Herne dropped to his hands and knees behind the altar, scuttling toward cover like an insect uncovered beneath a rock.

J.B. and Okie both fired their Mini-Uzis, handling the small guns almost as easily as if they were just pistols. Bodies spun and danced, carried by the streams of lead, tumbling to the chill stone tangled in frozen embraces.

During the firefight, time disappeared. Hours became minutes and minutes became seconds; seconds became shards of broken time. And one of those tiny shards stretched to a hundred lifetimes.

Ryan took his finger off the trigger, and looked around the open area between the buildings. Apart from four or five of the crazies who were moaning and crying for help, it was over.

"I'll take them," said Okie, stalking among the corpses, her boots splashing in blood. She set her blaster on single shot and, stooping and firing, put a round through the necks of all the wounded.

"Lori," ordered Ryan, "get Hennings untied and dressed. His clothes must be over there. Doc, go with her and keep watch. Might still be some of them around, and— That tall bastard, Herne, he's gone!"

"That way," said Krysty, her voice weak and strained. He spun around to see her leaning on the frame of the ruined door, her face as pale as parchment, a tiny thread of blood trickling from the corner of her mouth.

"Where? You all right?"

"Sure. Just...I heard him run. Like a rat in a cellar. That way, behind the cross on the wall."

A burst of fire made Ryan duck, but it was only J.B., wasting an elderly man who'd come tottering out of a hut, waving a great cleaver with a chipped edge.

"I will not stay here. This place is now soiled with blood. I shall lead my children from this valley of dark abomination into the plain of lightness."

The apostle, Ezekiel Herne, had appeared from behind a tumbledown wall, his hands stretched out, one of them gripping the obsidian knife. His eyes were blank and staring. A hideous parody of a smile hung on his lips.

Doc was on the far side of the altar, getting ready to cut Henn loose, and was directly in the line of fire, blocking Okie, J.B. and Ryan from shooting down the madman.

"Hit him, Doc," called Ryan.

"Use your cannon," added J.B.

"As I go, surely shall I not go alone," said Herne, drawing nearer to the old-timer. "This sacrifice shall be not maimed nor worthless."

"Do it, now," urged Okie.

"Bust him!" said Ryan quietly.

Like someone waking from a long dream, Doc Tanner began to fumble with the flap of the holster attached to his broad leather belt. But his fingers were cold, and it seemed to take an eternity.

Herne was so close in line that none of the others could take him out without risking Doc's life. Had the skeletal man been holding a blaster, none of them would have hesitated, even if it meant wiping Doc out at the same time. But a knife was a close-range threat.

The antique Le Mat was so heavy that Doc nearly dropped it as he clumsily thumbed the hammer back. Herne was almost on top of him, already raising the gleaming midnight blade just as he had when he'd been about to rip the living heart from Henn's body.

The pistol was adjusted to fire its .63-caliber shotgun round. Holding the pistol in both hands, Doc squeezed the trigger. There was a great burst of powder smoke and a boom like a stun gren exploding. Ryan saw the way that the Le Mat kicked high in the old man's grip, but at that range, with that sort of charge, he really couldn't miss.

The skinny preacher was thrown back by the impact. His black coat disappeared into tatters and rags, and a great fountain of blood sprayed out from him. He landed flat on his back, his knife flying high in the bright morning air. The shot had hit him in the center of the chest, pulping ribs, driving the razored splinters of bone into his heart and lungs, killing him instantly.

Some of his blood splashed onto the broken wall behind him. Ryan looked up at the tortured figure of the Christ on the cross. Its midnight sheen was now dappled with fresh crimson that ran down the anguished face, the thighs, the ankle stumps.

"Got the ace on the fuckin' line with that one, Doc," said Okie, grinning appreciatively.

The old man holstered the smoking pistol and turned away without saying a word.

Henn was almost gray with exposure, and it took a great blazing fire and much effort to bring some life back into his limbs. The shooting had awakened Finnegan, who came lurching outside just after Doc iced the leader of the crazies. Wiping the sleep from his bleary eyes, he asked, "What the fuck is goin' on?"

Henn eventually recovered, though there were numerous scratches and bites on his body, particularly around his thighs and the lower part of his belly. And his penis was scabbed and bloody from what looked like severe friction burns on it.

As soon as he was coherent and dressed, Ryan ordered everyone back to the buggies, ready to move.

Doc had walked off on his own and returned only now, when he heard the roar of the engines. He looked pale. Ryan took him to one side.

"You feelin'...you know, Doc? You did what you had to. That bastard would have opened you from...?"

"Thorax to pubis, Ryan. Yes, I know, but killing does not come easy to me."

"It's a craft you have to learn, Doc. Just like any other."

"Then I confess I will do my best. Ah..."

"What?"

"While walking there alone with my contemplations, I recalled something I had forgotten. I mentioned the word *crater* brought back memories. I have now managed to remember it."

"Go on."

"Chron-jumps."

"What the...?"

Doc looked around to make sure the others were not within hearing distance. "The gateways. You know they're mat-trans ports. You get in and instantly you're carried somewhere else."

"Yeah. Look, I'm fuckin' freezin' to the bone out here, Doc. Can't we...?"

"It won't take much longer, sir. I said that there had been some dreadful accidents. I didn't tell you because I couldn't remember it, but the gateways have also been used for other experiments. Chron-jumps. Time travel. It does work."

"Never. Come on, Doc. You know you get confused sometimes."

"Most of the time, my dear Mr. Cawdor. But here is a moment of crystal clarity. I know that time travel is a reality—I know better than any living soul, believe me. But they tried other times. Once, and once only it nearly worked."

Either Doc Tanner had completely lost all his creds, or he was telling the truth. Ryan shook his head, resisting the temptation to slap himself to see if he was dreaming all this.

"It is passing strange how I can fail to know even my right hand from my left and still recall some fragments of the past in such clarity. It was the sixth day of August in the year 1930. Seventy-one years before Armageddon. A man of great distinction got into a cab in what was called Manhattan, in old New York. He waved to a friend and disappeared forever."

"What's this got to do with talkin' about volcanoes and craters?"

"Wait. The men who ran the Gateway and the Cerberus projects were evil. Oh, such wickedness and misery! My dear, dear Emily! They were trawling and they picked up this man. I was there when he came through, or when what was left of him came through."

Ryan had enough sense not to interrupt Doc to ask who Emily was. That might have been enough to throw his memory off the subject forever.

"It nearly, so nearly proved a success. A justice of the supreme court. It would have... I can still see what came."

"Go on, Doc." Behind Ryan, the rest of the group had boarded the ice buggies and were watching curiously from the ob slits.

"A shirt with a high collar. I remember the shoes were very sharply pointed, which was the fashion of the time, and were polished like twin mirrors. The suit was double-breasted, a brown pinstripe. That was the expression, *pinstripe*. That torn suit—with the label of the tailor still neatly sewn within it."

Doc's voice was becoming quieter. The early sun had long gone and the day was turning colder and bleaker. Gray clouds streaked with a dull purple were gathering over the giant mountain behind them, and already the first flakes of threatening snow were blowing.

"Those clothes. And... most of his trousers were missing. All but the lower jaw of the head was gone. That row of white teeth, everything sliced clean as a razor, and very little blood. The right hand was there, perfect, the fingers still curling, but the left was hewn away by some unknown and unimagined power. The voice mewed like a kitten. I think that was the worst of it—that little, little mewing voice. Lord forgive us for what was done in the name of science and progress! Progress! That poor relic of a man, plucked from the past to end...who knows where? Or when?''

"But what's this got to do with craters, Doc? I don't see the connection.''

Doc's veiled eyes turned to him, unblinking. "The name of...''

J.B.'s shout interrupted them. "It's droppin' fast, Ryan. If we're goin', we should move. Goin' to be bad weather soon.''

"Sure, sure. Go on, Doc.''

"For...what? Go on? Ah, I comprehend you, Mr. Cawdor, indeed I do. Go on and get into those infernal internal combustion machines. Of course.''

It had gone. The call from the Armorer had been enough to tip Doc's mind back over the edge, from sanity into utter confusion. But even the few coherent sentences that Doc had managed gave Ryan plenty to think about. Time travel! Maybe the gateways could be used for time travel. That was something else.

THE SMALL BAROMETER in the cab of Buggy One told its own tale. The pointer moved down and down as they drove, roughly maintaining a heading that would take them toward Fairbanks. But the land had undergone massive upheavals and distortions. Also, they were driving in one of the worst blizzards that Ryan had ever seen: worse than anything he'd ever experienced in the Deathlands. Visibility was falling toward zero, and winds rocked the heavy vehicles.

In the end there was nothing to do but halt. In Buggy Two, J.B. was having problems with the ignition system, which was coughing and cutting out. With a wind-chill factor that lowered the temperature outside to around minus one hundred and thirty, there was no hope of getting out to do repairs.

During a brief lull in the blizzard, Ryan saw a geodesic dome to the left, with buildings and an old radar dish scattered around it. "Part of what they called the DEW line," he said to Krysty, pointing it out. "Early defense system."

"Did 'em a lot of good, lover."

"Yeah. And it looks like a dam up at the head of that valley." But the storm came screaming back again and visibility fell to zero.

IN MIDAFTERNOON the storm began to ease, with the wind fading away to a mere fifty miles an hour, and the snow stopping altogether. The barometer rose from the depths and the watery sun peeked through the chem clouds.

"Buggy One to Two and Three. You read?"

Both came back affirmative.

"Map shows steep valley a few miles ahead. We'll go on and check it out. Keep in contact. If you can't fix the ignition, J.B., then call us, and we'll return, or you can all pack into Buggy Three. Is there room?"

"Sure, Ryan. No sweat. We'll meet up in the opening to that canyon. Keep in touch."

As he was about to press the gas pedal, Ryan had a second thought and switched the radio back on. "Mebbe better if you come with us, J.B. Henn's the engine expert, and he's got Finn to help him out. Six in one of these babies could be too much. You come with us."

"How about taking Lori?"

"No. If we meet trouble ahead, I'd rather have you along, providin' you don't smoke one of your bastard cheroots in here."

So the transfer was made, and the ailing buggy was left in the charge of Henn and Finnegan, who were both now recovered from the effects of the drugged punch. Despite intermittent snow flurries, visibility was generally fair.

"We should be near that valley," said J.B., holding a handgrip to steady himself against the rocking and lurching of the buggy.

"How far'll we go?" asked Krysty.

"Far as it takes. Looks like what's left up here is a big round zero," said Ryan. "Mebbe go back to the redoubt in a day or so and try movin' to warmer places. That the way you figure it, J.B.?"

"Sure."

The bazooka shell exploded near enough to the vehicle that it stopped dead, tipping up and over. The concussion was shocking, sending the three occupants toppling into instant darkness.

RYAN CAWDOR WAS FIRST to recover. He blinked and opened his eye, aware of a shattering ache in his head. He could feel blood crusted around his ears from the force of the shell.

Someone was looming over him; a man, well built. He wore some sort of silver band around his forehead, with a large red stone at its center. And his eyes were a peculiar golden color.

"Has the agony somewhat abated?" asked Uchitel, pronouncing the words carefully.

Chapter Fifteen

THE TRADER'S RULES had been simple. If you got caught by hostiles, you played it close and careful. That meant saying nothing and acting dumb.

The Narodniki hadn't bothered to tie Ryan, J.B. and Krysty. While the trio were unconscious, the Narodniki had taken their weapons, leaving them helpless in the camp of heavily armed guerrillas.

Uchitel still believed that this desolate land must have its legendary wealth somewhere. It couldn't possibly be this poor. Not after all he'd read and seen in the old books. Somewhere, there were towering buildings that scraped the sky; beautiful women who offered themselves to every man. All of that and more, was here in America.

Uchitel's more robust approach to questioning prisoners hadn't worked, so—fortunately for Ryan, J.B. and Krysty—this time, he was trying a more friendly approach, for a while. And this trio was utterly different from any of the shit-eating peasants he'd seen so far in America.

They wore clean clothes that were almost like uniforms and were made of excellent material, Uchitel observed; and they were physically in good condition, particularly the tall man who'd lost an eye. He was honed like a fine blade. The woman with the scarlet hair was also in marvelous condition: it had taken all of Uchitel's persuasiveness to prevent some of his followers from immediately raping her. The short skinny man with the spectacles didn't seem so powerful, but when they'd searched him they'd found he was a walking arsenal, carrying concealed guns, knives and explosives.

Their guns—modern, well greased, with no shortage of ammo for them—were better than anything that the Narodniki had ever seen. Most of the blasters looked as if they'd just come from an armaments factory.

While the trio was unconscious, the band had gathered around them.

"Did I not tell you?" Uchitel had said to his followers. "Here is wealth beyond reckoning! They drive a truck that can move over ice and snow! They must have fuel for it! Who has seen such things?" Nobody answered. "And where there are three, then must there not be more? *Da*, there *must*. And their guns...their clothes... We are close, brothers and sisters, so close to more power and wealth than we have ever dreamed of."

"What if they are too powerful for us?" Urach had asked.

"We have seen these Americans—need the Narodniki fear such folk? Here are three of their best, at our mercy!"

And the Narodniki roared their approval of Uchitel's words.

Had his agony abated somewhat? The question confounded Ryan Cawdor...as did this stranger with the ornate headband and the golden eyes. Had that bang on the head made him delirious? Ryan remembered that O'Mara, the machine gunner from War Wag One, had once suffered a fearful crack to the skull and had thereafter boasted for days that he was the Trader's grandfather—and his grandmother, too.

Blinking his eye, Ryan realized that it was no blurred vision from a dream or nightmare before him, but something all too real.

It was night, and they were in a hollow protected from the biting wind by the slope of the land. Several fires, fuelled by pyrotabs, burned all around. To one side was the indistinct white shape of the buggy. It was tipped over. Ryan blinked and turned, and was relieved to see Krysty and J.B., both seemingly unhurt, though the Armorer was as white as the snow and had a bloody nose. But his chest was rising and falling steadily. Then Krysty moaned and, even as Ryan watched, put her hand to her head, opening her eyes.

"Where...?" she began.

"Don't talk," said Ryan, quickly. "We're prisoners."

"Silence!" ordered Uchitel, grinning at his success in finding the right word from his tattered phrase book.

The girl sat up, burying her head in her hands. "I feel sick," she said.

J. B. Dix now also recovered consciousness and sat up and looked around. He said nothing at first. Taking off his glasses, he polished them on his sleeve, then replaced them. Finally he retrieved his beloved fedora and placed it on his head.

He looked at Ryan without expression. "They say anything?"

"Not well—I think they're foreign. Have you seen their blasters?"

Uchitel was watching them, trying to catch what they were saying. He did not want to appear foolish before his fellows.

"Yeah. They all got the old Makarov nine-mil pistols with double-action triggers. A few of 'em are carryin' Dragunova sniper's rifles. Lot of Kalashnikovs and seven point six two sub-MGs, all Russian. Never seen any in the Deathlands, only in the old manuals. You heard 'em talk?"

"Not really. They don't look like us."

Many of the faces were Oriental: slanted eyes, sallow complexions, straggly beards and long, black moustaches. The four or five women visible had coarse features and large hands. Not one of them looked at all like a mutie.

Almost all of them looked like vicious murderers.

"Can you offer us service?" asked Uchitel, looking from face to face.

"What?" said Ryan.

"We are lost and desire directions."

"Who are you?" he asked the tall Russian.

Uchitel turned the pages of his book with laborious slowness.

"Ah. Who are you?" he repeated. Pointing to his chest, he said, "Uchitel." Then, widening the gesture to include the rest of the band, he added, "We are Narodniki."

"I'm Ryan Cawdor. This is Krysty Wroth. And this is J. B. Dix."

Beneath him, Ryan felt the earth tremble, as though some immeasurably huge animal had stirred in its sleep. The guerrillas wore thick furs, with hoods of leather and gauntlets of fur-trimmed hide. From the maps that they'd seen in the redoubt, Ryan knew that Russia had been very close to the old United States in this region, being almost within sight of the coast of Alaska. But there had been no sign that the Russians had ever crossed the ice as invaders.

"It is a great pleasure to make your acquaintance," said Uchitel, stumbling over the last word.

"Talks like Doc, doesn't he?" said Krysty. "Like from the old times. Back in Harmony, I read books and that's how they talked. Mebbe that's what that book is. It helps him talk to us.''

Ryan nodded. "Must be, since it seems none of them speak our language. But watch it, it could be a trick."

There was another minor tremor, this time accompanied by a faint rumbling of the earth. The flames in the fires danced as if some invisible giant had blown on them. Some of the horses whinnied in alarm, and several of the Russians looked uneasily at one another. It was fast growing dark, and the wind was carrying sharp flakes of ice in its teeth.

Stamping his booted feet on the ground, Bochka, the Barrel, muttered something to Britva, who was at his side. Uchitel looked angrily toward him. "You fear a small shake of the earth, Bochka? It would take a large crack to swallow you up."

The others laughed, but not with conviction. The leader turned again to the three prisoners. Their weapons were piled by his feet, and he pointed down at them. "Good," he said. "I wish a further supply, if you please. Or I shall be forced to complain to your superior or manager or floor walker."

It was one of the most bizarre episodes in Ryan Cawdor's life—a life that was well studded with bizarre experiences.

He considered whether to say that they had many powerful friends in the area. But if he did that, the Russians might ambush the others, and they would all end up being wiped out. He decided it was safer to pretend they were alone and take the consequences of such admitted weakness.

"We have no more guns."

There was a delay while Uchitel translated and digested that. *"Nyet,"* he said, shaking his head. "Where are guns?"

"No," replied Ryan, standing up, stretching his legs. Krysty and J.B. also rose. All around them was a general movement of guns, muzzles edging in their direction. Putting up any kind of fight would be utterly suicidal.

"Give gun. Not gun, I give—" he found what he wanted on a page headed At The Hospital "—bad pain."

"No guns. These are all we have. No more."

Uchitel was becoming angry. Yet again, his careful plan was falling apart. These Americans were either poor and stupid or wealthy and stupid. At least these three had good clothes and guns, and the truck held all manner of treasures. He beckoned for Pechal to come to him.

"I want—" he began.

But Sorrow interrupted him. "The girl, Uchitel. Let me do the girl! Her hair is so—"

"Nyet. Not her. The man with the glasses. The others will watch."

Ryan and the others watched the exchange, guessing from the expressions on the men's faces what was going down. The gray-clad Russian with the soft voice had been licking his lips and staring at Krysty, rubbing his fingers together—long, strong fingers with long, hooked nails.

"Bad news time," said Ryan.

"Yeah," agreed J.B.

"He tell us guns where." Uchitel pointed at the Armorer and rattled off orders to his men to bind him. In moments J.B.'s hands were tied tightly behind his back, and he was brought to his knees and held there. Two dozen guns covered Ryan and Krysty.

"Are they going to torture him?" asked the girl.

"Seems they want guns like these. Must have come over as a raidin' party."

"Take my glasses off for me, Ryan," called J.B. "Don't want these stupes to break 'em. Had 'em for eight years. Don't know how I'd get on without 'em."

Watched by the Russians, Ryan did as J.B. asked, folding the glasses and putting them in his top pocket. The beardless Pechal moved in close to the kneeling man, looking down into his eyes. He touched J.B. on the side of the cheek with a forefinger, and the little man winced despite himself.

"Tell guns," said Uchitel.

"There aren't any more fuckin' guns you stupe bastard killer," shouted Ryan.

Uchitel nodded to Pechal.

Ryan watched, his face set like stone; the girl looked away. Pechal began gently, almost caressing the helpless J.B. He touched and pinched, twisting the soft, tender skin behind the ears and along the inside of the upper thigh. His nails dug into the Armorer's lips, pulling them until blood filled J.B.'s mouth and he spat it out in a fine spray over the Russian.

"Where guns?" asked Uchitel.

Ryan looked at him, his face showing none of the hatred and anger he felt. "I'll tell you this, you blood-eyed dog. You're fuckin' dead, friend. You're walkin' around, but you are dead as a spent bullet."

"What?"

Ryan shook his head in disgust. Krysty shuffled closer to him. "What can we do?"

"Nothin', lover. They got all the blasters. Man has the firepower, he gets to call the game. We watch and wait. Any half chance, take it and get the fuck out. Henn and the others must be comin' close. Head for 'em. That's all I can say."

Uchitel stepped in and swung an open palm across Ryan's face, knocking him on his back. Ryan sat there a moment, his head spinning from the blow, which had loosened one of his teeth. As Ryan got up, a lopsided smile came to his angular face.

"Do the same for you one day, cocksuckin' double-scarred bastard."

"Not talk. Talk guns. No pain."

The third earth tremor was vastly more powerful than the two minor quakes they'd felt earlier.

Ryan staggered sideways, retaining his balance only with effort. Nearly everyone was thrown off their feet. All the fires were shaken out, buried under a mist of ice and snow.

The air filled with a dreadful thundering roar and with so much dirt that it was difficult to breathe or see.

Ryan grabbed the girl by the arm. "Got to get J.B. Now."

There was a second quake, more violent than the first. It knocked both Ryan and Krysty off their feet. But Ryan's sense of direction and ice-cold nerve kept them going. Stumbling over bodies lying on the earth, they reached J.B., and Ryan knelt, still holding Krysty by her right hand.

"Took your fuckin' time, partner," said J.B., his voice as calm as if they were strolling across a summer meadow.

"Knife?"

"Right boot. They didn't find it."

Ryan slid his fingers inside the high combat boot, feeling the taped hilt of a small knife. Pulling it from the sheath, he used it to slice through the ropes that bound J.B.

As the last cord fell away, J.B. rose to his feet, leaning on Ryan. "Thanks. That bastard, that swift and evil fucker had hard hands."

The ground still moved. It was like being on War Wag One when it drove at speed along an old concrete highway in the Deathlands. A steady vibration.

"Get the blasters," said J.B. "That way."

Despite the darkness and confusion, they moved straight to the pile of guns and knives. Each of them grabbed what they could, holstering and sheathing their weapons. Ryan was still holding the long steel panga when someone grabbed him from behind.

"Fireblast!" he cursed, struggling to free his arms from the bearlike grip. But the man was strong, and it took all of Ryan's agility and cunning to free his right hand so that he could jab behind him with the point of the blade. Despite all the layers of fur that the Russian was wearing, the panga penetrated. There was a grunt of pain, the hold was loosened, and Ryan twisted his body clear. Then he turned and swung the blade as hard as he could, feeling it jar and crunch as it hit the man's ribs. In the cold he was aware of the flood of heat across his hand from the wound.

As the staggering figure screamed something in Russian—it had to be a call for aid—Ryan pushed the man away and turned to where he'd last seen Krysty and J.B.

"You there?"

"Yeah," said J.B.

"Here," said Krysty, unable to keep her voice from trembling. All around them, the guerrillas were running and yelling. Across the camp someone fired a pistol four times. They heard a yelp of pain.

"South," said Ryan. "Keep close. Kill anythin' that moves if it's not us."

"Why not get the radio from the buggy?" asked the girl.

"No time. Got to move. There's thirty or more of 'em. We know where Henn and the others are headed. We'll meet up with 'em."

The earthquake was continuing with waves of varying power that made the ice-bound pebbles shift and rattle.

Ryan Cawdor was in the lead, Krysty slipped and stumbled behind him, and J.B. brought up the rear. Something loomed in front of him, and he slashed at it with the panga, then realized too late it was one of the terrified ponies, rearing and kicking. The steel opened a deep gash along its shoulder, but one of its front hooves caught Ryan a glancing blow on the arm. At that moment, the earth gave its strongest convulsion yet, and the ground beneath him rose eighteen inches or more.

He slipped and rolled forward, feeling snow all around him. A boulder hit him on the knee, making him yell with sudden pain. As he whirled down the slope he heard screams from behind, and men calling in Russian.

His mouth filled with powdery snow, and he coughed and choked as he rolled. With an effort, he managed to spread his arms and legs into a star shape, checking his slide down the hill.

The tremor passed, and he sat up, checking his blasters. His long coat was torn, his knee hurt, and there was a dull throbbing where the horse had kicked him. He could taste blood from a cut near his mouth.

But he was alive.

The patch over his missing left eye had shifted and he tugged it back in place. He stood, trying to determine where he was. He was at the bottom of a steep ravine, with water a few inches deep under his boots.

He'd fallen a couple of hundred feet and had no idea where Krysty and J.B. were. There were Russians all around, blundering in the darkness.

Ryan was alone with no food, no water and no way to keep warm in a land he didn't know, with a night to face with temperatures that might drop to seventy or eighty below.

Survival was going to be hard.

Chapter Sixteen

ONE OF THE TRADER'S SAYINGS came to Ryan as he moved cautiously through the stygian gloom away from the camp of the Russian butchers.

"The will to live is quite simply a matter of your personal courage."

One of the things that the Trader had always insisted on was each war wag having a number of experts: on explosives or first aid or food or armaments or driving—or survival. Finnegan had been the survival expert. Trader had spent a lot of time lecturing Finnegan, using old manuals and books, drilling into him what should be done in heat or cold or a nuke attack or an ambush, a flood or a fire or a fall. In turn, every few weeks, Finnegan would give a talk to the rest of the crew—as would the other experts, checking that everyone knew what to do.

Now, kneeling in the slush, feeling it soaking through his trousers, Ryan recalled some of the things that Finn had told them.

Panic was the biggest threat. Fear made a man move too fast in the wrong direction. He should stop if he could and draw a breath.

Ryan stood, fighting to control his breathing, still hearing the ground rumbling miles below his feet. Also catching the sound of the Russians, running and calling. Now he saw a couple of flaming torches as they started to search for their lost prisoners. He guessed that J.B. and Krysty, if they'd stayed together, would be making for the south to meet with the others. But his fall had put him on the wrong side of the enemy. Now he'd have to try and loop around.

Ryan took stock. Guns and ammo, check. Clothes and knives, check. Health, bruises here and there but nothing too threatening: check. Compass, check. Food and drink.

"No," he said to himself.

Nor heat.

The land was so barren that his chances of finding food were remote. But he knew from experience that he could exist for several days without food, even in the bitter cold. But he had to drink. He stooped and cupped some of the water around his feet, tasting it cautiously. The fact that it was flowing and not frozen was a sign that it originated higher up—probably near the dam that he'd spotted earlier—and had been melted by heat from a volcano. The taste was bitter, iron with a dash of sulfur. If he could drink now and fill his belly, it would last him a couple of days.

If he didn't find the others after a couple of days in the lingering nuclear winter, then he was going to be dead anyway.

He knelt and lapped like a dog, lifting his head every now and again to peer into the gloom. At the bottom of the steep valley he was sheltered from the bitter wind, but he knew that he couldn't stay there long. The Russians would be searching. Judging from what he'd seen of him, their amber-eyed leader wasn't the sort of man who gave up easily.

Far above Ryan, there was a burst of automatic fire that raked the far side of the ravine, bullets ricocheting and whining into the darkness. Someone shouted and Ryan ducked, huddling against the cold rock, wearing his hood so that his face wouldn't show white.

But the shooting wasn't repeated, and the voices moved toward the south. The earth finally ceased shaking, and all he could hear was the faint whistling of the wind.

"Time to move," he said.

BACK IN THE DEATHLANDS, winter had been a time of bitter hardship, with blizzards and fiercely low temperatures. But here in Alaska the long nuclear winter still had the land in its thrall. In places there were deep snowbanks that had been piled up by the endless winds, and in other places, just bare rock, scoured and shattered by permafrost. Gray and dull green lichens clung precariously to the more sheltered places, but life was almost extinct, clinging to the edges of an abyss.

Either a man found protection or he tried to keep moving. After an hour of walking steadily west and then curving cautiously back toward the south, Ryan was feeling exhausted. Much of the time he was battling against a shrieking gale that plucked at his hood, blasting splinters of ice into his eye. Such a buffeting soon cuts away at the senses of even the strongest man. It becomes difficult to think rationally, and all a man wants is to lie down and rest a little, just sleep for a few minutes.

A few long, long, long minutes.

Ryan tried to keep moving, without going too fast. He remembered that Finn had urged care. To sweat was to lose body heat; to lose body heat was, eventually, to die. He knew the signs of frostbite: small, gray-yellow patches on the skin, accompanied by numbness, later leading to the blackening of gangrene and finally to death. That was something he didn't need to fear. Either he'd find the others in the next day or so, or he'd be dead anyway.

To counter the cold on his face, Ryan exercised his muscles, alternately scowling and smiling, so that his cheeks wouldn't freeze and lose all sensation. He checked the small chron on his wrist, finding that he'd been away from the Russians for nearly three hours. Unless they scattered, he figured he was safe from stumbling back into their arms. Once, he heard the distant sound of gunfire. It lasted only a few seconds and wasn't repeated.

With little light, it was hard going. He was constantly slipping and falling, slogging on, pausing now and again to listen. Once there was the sound of running water, but it seemed to come from his left, away from the direction he'd taken.

Ryan knew all the survival tricks of lighting a life-saving blaze using a lens, or even by taking apart a couple of bullets to ignite tinder or paper. But in that desert of ice and stone there was nothing he could burn. No wood at all.

"Shelter," he said, panting hard. A pale sliver of moon danced above him, occasionally visible through the shreds of high, gray clouds. It gave enough light for him to see a big drift of snow banked against the overhanging lip of a ridge of rough stones a hundred paces ahead of him.

With his panga, he began to carve the white bank, cutting eighteen-inch cubes, stacking them to make a wall to break the wind. He worked steadily, creating a tunnel, gradually expanding it until it was large enough for him to climb into. The wall of snow bricks, which had grown higher and higher as he'd carved out the tunnel, was arranged around the entrance. If he'd had better tools, he could have tried to make a full house of snow, or "igloo," as Finn had called it. But he also remembered that there was a danger of such places melting and caving in, trapping the occupants.

Ryan sat down, making sure his coat was tucked beneath him. Immediately he was aware of the shelter that his snow cave provided against the weather. Out of the gale, there was no longer the bitter numbness in his face. Every few minutes he stood up and shuffled his feet, swinging his arms to keep his circulation going.

Around five in the morning, he dozed for a while, waking when the first light of dawn came sliding over the eastern mountains.

"FEELS LIKE A STONE buried in your flesh," Ryan muttered. He was again slogging relentlessly onward in a great loop south, hoping to meet the others.

His toes hurt and he could feel a faint prickling on his exposed face. His hands were also becoming swollen and tender.

"Stone in your flesh," he repeated. That was how Finnegan had described what the early symptoms of frostbite felt like.

It was nearly midday, but the temperature seemed to be dropping. Off to the north, he could see a great smear of yellow across the sullen sky, where a volcano was erupting. At the top of a ridge, he stared out through the swirling wall of snow, looking for any sign of life, friendly or otherwise. He thought he saw the great dish of the radar installation many miles ahead, but it seemed impossible to reach before evening. And he was beginning to doubt his ability to survive another night without proper shelter and some food.

THE MUTIE POLAR BEAR came blundering out of the mists of evening, padding on huge, shaggy paws. Ryan was close to the limits of exhaustion and hunger. His concentration was slipping. Still, he plodded onward, trying to make as much ground as he could before hacking another shelter from the unyielding snow.

"Fuckin' fireblast!" he cursed, stumbling back a few paces, leveling the Heckler & Koch G12 at the hulking beast that stood less than twenty paces away. Its red eyes glared at him; breath plumed from its jaws. For a few moments, man and beast stared at each other, neither sure of the other's intentions.

"Just fuck off out of my way," said Ryan, finger on the trigger of the automatic rifle.

The creature moved its head back and forth, almost as if trying to hypnotize its intended prey with the regular pendulum swinging.

Saliva dripped from the long, tusked teeth. The head moved faster and still faster. Ryan blinked, fighting against tiredness to hold the gun steady, knowing that one lapse of concentration would be fatal.

Noticing a sudden tensing of the hump of muscle across the bear's shoulders and guessing it presaged a charge, he didn't hesitate any longer. The gun set on continuous fire, he squeezed the trigger, bracing his hip against the recoil. In a crosswind the 4.7 mm bullet was liable to a degree of drift, though the trajectory drop was excellent.

At twenty paces, the stream of bullets tore into the polar bear, bursting its heavy skull apart. Ryan kept firing into the animal's broad chest, sending it staggering to its knees, then onto its side. Its feet kicked and flailed in the bloodied snow. Ryan used the entire fifty-round magazine, knowing that a beast of that size needed to be terminated with utmost prejudice and speed. There wouldn't have been a second chance.

He reloaded, looking into the gloom of the onrushing night. The sound of the gun would have been so brief that he doubted there was any danger from the Russians.

Its head blasted to pulp, the bear was undeniably dead. But as Ryan bent to touch it, feeling the warmth of the carcass, he was startled to feel the heart still pumping, even though there was virtually no blood left in the whole monstrous body.

He took off his gauntlets, pushing his hands inside the gaping chest cavity, careful to avoid scratches from the jagged ribs and breastbone. The scarlet pool around his feet was steaming. Finn had come out once with a horror story of some trader up in the north, dying of the cold, who'd shot a buffalo on the high plains, hacked its belly open, ripped out the guts and crawled into the carcass and huddled there in the glorious warmth. But during the night, the cold had frozen the soft flesh to an immovable stiffness, and he wasn't able to get out.

And so perished.

Ryan was content to have his hands and arms warmed, feeling inside for the rhythmic pounding of the bear's heart. He brought his smoking fingers to his mouth and licked the salty blood. His stomach heaved with revulsion for a few moments, but he fought against the sickness, lapping at the clotting crimson liquid, taking as much nourishment as he was able.

He sliced away a few thin pieces of the meat, chewing with a grim determination, forcing himself to swallow. Then he took more. From previous experiences of hunger, he knew that to eat too much, particularly such rich meat, would only make him throw up.

The blood dried and began to freeze on his hands, cracking and falling off in dark brown flakes. Ryan rubbed his hands together to remove as much of the blood as possible and felt his circulation reviving. Night was now very close, and it was time once more to build a shelter.

This time there was less snow, and he was forced to struggle with boulders, painstakingly chipping them free of the ice with his panga, piling them into a wall, filling in the cracks with snow.

It wasn't solid enough.

After a couple of hours he began to feel the telltale signs of the biting cold. His feet and hands were growing numb and he was becoming drowsy. It wasn't the usual, healthy desire for sleep after a hard day; it was an insidious, creeping sleeplessness, offering a tempting promise of warmth and relief from pain. It was overlaid with the feeling that he'd done his best and had now earned his rest.

"Fuck that!" said Ryan.

He stood, stamping his feet, pulling up the hood around his ears, then changing his mind and lowering it once more. If he was going to start walking this night, he would be virtually blind. It would be madness to make himself virtually deaf by covering his ears with the hood.

He had decided that his only genuine hope of surviving was to make for the old ruined radar station with its conspicuous geodesic dome. There might be shelter there. And it was the obvious place for Henn and the others to wait for him.

Every few minutes the moon broke through the low clouds, throwing the land into sharp relief. The track toward the tumbled buildings wandered like a drunk man, gradually coming down off the wind-torn edge of the escarpment. Ryan's guess was that his destination was about four miles off. At his best normal pace on level ground, that would take him under an hour.

After three exhausting hours he was still less than halfway there.

He began to hallucinate.

Once he saw the Trader. He stood a few yards ahead of Ryan, pointing an accusing finger. His lips moved but Ryan couldn't hear the words. Just a little while later, he fell and slipped into the blackness. His mind told him that he had broken some teeth in the fall, and he reached inside his mouth and found splintered fragments of teeth awash in blood along with feathery pieces of crumpled blue plastic. Yet it seemed to him that this was a perfectly normal thing to find inside his mouth.

Once, on a ridge parallel to the one where he staggered onward, Ryan thought he saw a pack of lean hunting wolves, all facing him, their slavering jaws glittering in the moonlight. The leader was a huge creature, standing as high as a man's chest. Then the pack vanished behind some boulders. Ryan was not certain they'd been there in the first place.

Dawn brought a spectacular sky of orange and yellow streaked with fiery crimson. But Ryan Cawdor scarcely noticed it.

His snospex were in the ice buggy; without them, his sight was deteriorating. His eye felt full of grit, and everything seemed to be tinted red and was blurred with shadows. But he was closing in on the radar station. Behind him, to the left, he could make out the silhouette of the huge dam, dominating the plain and valleys beneath it.

The night's cold had struck deep, and he kept stumbling. He lost one of his gloves on the descent from the ridge, and his left hand was bruised and swollen. His knees and ribs hurt, as did a cut along his jaw from the jagged edge of a black boulder.

He entered a shallow dip, and for several minutes the radar station was out of sight. When he emerged, it was a scant quarter mile off across level ground.

Ryan knew then that he was going to make it.

Despite his dimmed vision, he suddenly made out a group of people hurrying toward him. They were shouting and waving, but he couldn't quite hear the words. Now, so close to safety, Ryan was able to let go. He slipped wearily to his knees. Finally, like a tired man entering deep water, he slid forward on his face, waiting for the others to come to him.

Chapter Seventeen

A LOUD CLICKING SOUND, echoing, becoming louder and louder. A threatening, insistent noise that seemed as if it were drilling into Ryan's brain.

The sound became almost deafening.

And stopped.

"What . . . ?" he began. "What the fuck was that poundin' noise?"

"What noise?"

"Clicking. Metal on stone?"

"The heels of my boots in the corridor," replied Krysty Wroth.

"Sounded like hammers in my head. How long did I sleep this time?"

She sat beside him on the battered metal bed, her long hair tied back with a strip of black ribbon. "I guess about an hour, lover. Altogether, today, around seven hours. It was just after dawn when I heard you comin' and we came out to carry you in. You were near the end, Ryan."

"I know it. Where's J.B.?"

"Gone to visit the ghost town by the dam. You remember him tellin' you?"

Ryan sat up, feeling bone weary but for the first time, realizing that he was safe and well. They'd given him warm soup and a light brown alcoholic liquid that tasted of burned wood and blazed in his throat as he swallowed it.

"I recall you tellin' me how you and J.B. fought your way clear, killed three or four of them Russians, then headed here and met up with Henn. The two buggies are both runnin' okay now, right?"

Krysty nodded. "Yeah. I wanted to stay and look for you. J.B. said no."

"He was right. In that sort of situation, I'd have left him."

"He's up with Okie and Doc. They radioed they'd found a town in a valley by the dam. They've got a missile up there."

Ryan swung his legs over the side of the bed, standing unsteadily, waving away the girl's helping hand. "No, I'm— Missile? What sort?"

She shook her head. "J.B. said it was experimental. Reeled off a load of reference letters and numbers that didn't mean anything to him."

"Can it be . . . ?"

"Blasted off? Yeah. There's a launcher. Oh, an' J.B. says there's a dummy one, as well, without any launch motor or explosive—just a shell."

"Is he comin' back here today?"

"No. Said you were to rest up. We've got food and heat and all. Lori's been sniveling with a cold. I think we should have left her at the redoubt, Ryan."

"She'd have died. She saved us from that bloody-minded old bastard, Quint. She's not used to the outside, that's all."

"You figure those killers are comin' after us, Ryan?" asked Krysty.

"That quake must have scattered their ponies. It'll take 'em a day or more to get together. But . . . yeah, I guess that yellow-eyed shitter was interested enough in us to come this way. Round about tomorrow noon, we could have us a real firefight. It'd be better if we were all together, so let's go join the others."

THE SEVERE QUAKES that had opened the earth around the camp of the Narodniki, delaying them in their southerly push, had barely been felt by the pursuing militia, who were on the far side of a range of low hills.

It had enabled them to close the gap on the guerrillas. And the closer they got, the faster they moved.

Major Zimyanin sat on his horse, peering ahead. Ice hung from the stiff points of his long moustache. He removed his fur cap with its single silver circle and wiped his bald head with a fur glove. His pockmarked face was less gloomy than usual.

All the signs indicated that they were catching up with the band of killers. They'd found the raggled, frozen corpses that Uchitel and his group had left as silent testimonials to their brutality: bodies so torn by the wolves and other scavengers that it was hard to tell the manner of their passing. But some still showed the marks of burning or of the knife or the bullet.

The cavalry patrol had seen identical marks in the hamlet of Ozhbarchik on the other side of the frozen Bering Strait.

During a day-long blizzard, the major had felt the unhappiness of his troops, many of whom were muttering for a return to their homes in Magadan. But he had urged them on with promises of extra pay all around and hints that the best troopers might be promoted and transferred to the West. He knew from bitter experience that it was pointless to appeal either to their religion or, even worse, to their loyalty to the party.

But now they were close, anticipating an actual sighting of their prey within the next twenty-four hours.

Aliev, the Mongolian tracker with the hideously mutilated face, was excited. Jumping, green snot dripping from the raw hole where his nose should have been, he held up his right hand, showing only one finger, indicating a single day. Then he chopped at it with the edge of his left hand, showing he thought that the Narodniki were even less than a day ahead of them.

Zimyanin stood in the stirrups, using one of his most valuable possessions—a pair of scratched and battered binoculars with the name Zeiss engraved on the side. He knew of no other officer of his rank who possessed such a wonderful tool. Many had cheap telescopes or binoculars, but nothing to compare with these.

To the south, in a cleft in the mountains, he could see a great wall of concrete, with a stream of water gushing from near its top. It had to be some sort of dam, he figured, blocking a river that was kept ice free by some underground source of heat.

He moved the glasses to the right and inspected a series of sharp-edged valleys. He thought he could see a trail worming into one of the valleys. For a moment, Zimyanin thought he could even see signs of life: a plume of snow, as though men on horse-back moved there, and tiny black specks against the whiteness.

But his hands began to tremble, and the glass blurred with his breath. By the time he wiped the lenses clear, the figures had gone.

If they'd ever been there in the first place.

AVALANCHES HAD DESTROYED virtually all of the little mining town that had once flourished high in the ravine near the looming dam. Now only a few roofless shacks remained.

Ryan and the others had discussed their plans, finally agreeing that the Russian guerrillas were too dangerous to ignore. In the morning they would take the buggies and return to the redoubt. Then they would use the gateway to leave the ice-bound desert of Alaska behind them.

Chapter Eighteen

OKIE WAS ON GUARD, walking cautiously around the ruined houses at the neck of the valley. From below she heard the river tumbling over the rounded stones at the foot of the dam's spillway. To her right, she could make out the great dam, with its towers and pumping stations. The moon gave only a pale, spectral light, not enough to illuminate the trail that clung to the mountainside, dappled with patches of ice and snow. It hadn't been easy to negotiate that trail, even with the tracked buggies, but there was no other way up or down.

Her low-heeled tan riding boots clicked on the loose stones. The Mini-Uzi was safely in its holster on her belt; the M-16 carbine cradled in her arms. Looking behind her, she saw the tiny ruby glow of the fire that smoldered at the center of their camp between the two parked buggies. Straining her eyes, the blaster could see the gravelike mounds that were her sleeping comrades. The larger one was Ryan Cawdor and the mutie girl tangled together.

Okie spat, her sullen face showing her dislike for Krysty Wroth. Ryan had shown interest in her before the redhead had appeared. If anything happened to the mutie...?

There was always the strong possibility of a nasty accident.

She turned slowly, feeling the wind tugging at her long dark ponytail. Behind her she caught the sound of stones shifting, as if a piece of frozen earth had slithered down the hill. Okie whirled, finger on the trigger of her carbine.

For a few moments, she stood there, still as a statue, ears straining for any odd sound.

It was repeated.

It came from her right, where an old concrete sluice hung perilously over the side of the valley, stretching up into the darkness. If anything were to happen to it, then the whole tangle of stone and metal would come grinding down on the sleeping camp.

Okie moved slowly, keeping to the shadows, gun questing ahead of her. She placed each step with utmost care, as silent as a lover's touch on velvet skin.

Her ears caught the frail scraping of metal on metal. She stopped, letting her eyes rake around the ghost town—drawing a slow breath as she saw them. Three. No, four. One stooped over by the foot of the sluice's main support girders. The others ringed him, facing her.

Okie raised her gun to shoulder level, bracing it, squinting down the barrel. She tightened her finger on the trigger.

The explosion woke the night. The M-16 spat out death, empty cartridge cases tinkling on the stones. She saw the bursting sparks as the 5.56 mm bullets bounced off the rocks and the iron, screeching into the dark valley. Two of the four strangers went down under the first hail of lead. The third dived sideways, snapping off shots from a Kalashnikov AKM, the heavy 7.62 mm bullets whining high over Okie's head, dashing splinters of rock around her.

The fourth figure vanished into the maze of twisted metal. Okie's guess was that the fourth man who had been crouched over the girders, was an explosives expert. If she was right, then he was the prime target. She waited, knowing that the third blaster was likely to try for better cover.

He did.

She bowled him over in a jumble of kicking legs and scrabbling hands.

There was no need for her to warn Ryan and the others. At the first echo of the hammering carbine, they were awake. Within seconds they were beside her, holding their weapons. Lori and Doc were the last to show.

"Cover me!" yelled Okie, making her move—a dodging, crouched run toward the spot where the fourth man had disappeared.

Ryan and J.B. both gave scattering fire, raking the hillside to right and left of the darting girl. Hennings and Finnegan were behind them, taking shelter behind an overturned water tank. The four men hadn't come raiding alone. Already there was spasmodic fire from farther down the trail, but it was poorly aimed.

The big man who'd gone into hiding was Grom; nicknamed Thunder, he was the expert in the gang on all manner of bombs, mines and explosives. Uchitel had sent him in with a small support party to try to bring the sluice down on the sleeping Americans. Nobody had seen Okie, patrolling like a panther in the shadows.

Grom was deaf and hadn't heard the opening burst of fire, but he'd seen his friends falling. Now he was on his own, with the long-haired woman after him. He held a parcel of plastic explosives, primed and attached to a timer. But there was a manual override on the bomb. He saw that he was trapped, but he grinned; he could still set off his bomb and take these Americans with him in death. With Uchitel as his leader, he feared failure much more than mere death.

Someone farther down the trail fired a phos gren, flooding the whole area with a stark white light. It flushed the lurking Russian from his hiding place, sending him scampering toward the blind corner of the trail. He clutched the bomb to his chest like an undelivered birthday present. Okie spotted him and fired from the hip, the bullets lancing through the dirt all round the Russian. Miraculously Grom wasn't hit, though he stumbled and fell, nearly dropping the bomb.

Okie, lusting to kill, dropped the empty M-16. Not bothering to draw her machine pistol from its holster, she went for the cowering man with only her long-bladed Italian stiletto.

Ryan was about to shoot at the Russian, when he saw the danger of hitting the girl. Also, as clear as day in the light of the phos gren, he saw the man fumbling with the parcel.

"Fireblast!" he spat. "He's primin' a fuckin' bomb." He raised his voice to warn Okie. "Watch it! He's got a bastard bomb!"

If the blaster heard him, she gave no sign of it. Never deviating from her attack, she launched herself at the Russian like an arrow. Grom saw her coming and held up the package of explosives as though it were some holy relic that warded off evil.

"So long," said J. B. Dix quietly, so that only Ryan heard him.

As usual, the little man was right.

Grom's intention had been to throw the bomb toward Ryan and the others, but Okie's unexpected attack thwarted that. He was taken so much by surprise that he was still holding the ticking bomb as she landed on him.

The knife struck with practiced, lethal accuracy high at the side of the deaf man's neck, just below his right ear, opening the carotid artery in a spouting gush of crimson. Grom was dying as he fell. His last act was to grab the girl's green sweater, clutching her to him in his death spasm.

Before she could free herself, the bomb exploded.

The heavy sound was muffled by the two bodies. Ryan ducked, feeling the shock wave tug his dark hair. The booming noise echoed across the valley, bouncing flatly off the dam. When he stood up, his face was wet with gore, and he felt sickened at the sound of human flesh landing all around him. A thin pall of smoke blew across the plateau by the ghost town, then was gone. The rising wind carried with it all trace of the woman whose name had been Okie.

UCHITEL SIGNALED THE REST of the attacking party to retreat. With the element of surprise gone and his party whittled down to only nineteen men and four women, he couldn't risk a frontal assault and an all-out firefight farther up the hillside where the massive dam loomed over them, dominating the valley. They assembled at a spot where the river ran fast and narrow, barely fifteen feet wide, with a thin veil of gray ice growing at its edges.

"What now?" asked Urach.

"They can go nowhere. There is the one road, and we control that here by the river. We have them trapped, my brother. Let us wait and they will come to us and beg us for mercy.''

His comrades bellowed with laughter.

"SHORT AN' CURLIES, Ryan," said J.B.

"What?" said Finnegan.

"Those bastards got us by the short and curlies. No other road out or in. We go down, and they pick us off like flies in molasses."

"Mebbe not," said Ryan.

"I have never ceased to wonder at the enigmatic nature of your discourse in moments of dire stress," Doc said, sitting against a stone wall that still carried a faded advertisement for a canned beer.

"What's the idea, Ryan?" asked J.B.

Lori moved beside Ryan, staring wonderingly into his face. "We live?" she asked.

"Sure. We live right up to the moment that we start dyin'," he replied. Turning to the Armorer, he said, "This missile you found..."

THE LAUNCHER was like a sledge. The red-and-white missile rested on the sledge, with torn strips of tarpaulin swaddling it like a baby. J.B. and Finn peeled away the covering, revealing the sleek, elegant shape. It was about the length of a tall man and had four triangular fins at the rear.

There were letters and numbers stenciled on the casing, black on white, and white on red: USAF A/

T/M SD4 TRD/C 24942 1/1/00. And in a circle, with arrows pointing to it, there was the single word Active.

"There's another one without *active* on it," J.B. pointed out. "This could take out a dozen war wags in one go. Never seen a baby this size still juiced an' ready to go."

"But it's not a lot of good against the scattering of Russians down by the river. It's not antipersonnel, is it?"

They all stood around the launching cradle. Ryan noticed that someone—now long dead and turned to dust—had scrawled the girl's name, Cathy, on the live missile in green paint. For a moment he wondered who she'd been.

IT WAS TEMPTING to do it in the dark. The effect would be more terrifying, the shock more total. But in the end J.B. agreed with Ryan that it would be best to wait until first light.

The party split up. J.B. stayed in the narrow valley with Doc and Lori. Ryan, Henn, Finn and Krysty moved carefully down the track, stopping about one hundred and fifty feet above where Uchitel and the Narodniki commanded the river crossing.

"Could hit their horses there," whispered Finnegan, pointing to the shifting blur of the Russians' animals.

"Tell 'em we're here? No. No fuckin' way. We just stop here and wait and watch. We move when the time comes."

MAJOR ZIMYANIN was also watching the river crossing. His cavalry unit was a scant couple of miles off on the far side of the valley. He lay on a promontory of cold rock. The sniper, Corporal Solomentsov, was beside him. The party didn't allow muties in the fighting patrols—indeed, they were unofficially being purged—and Solomentsov's eyesight was so good that the major suspected that he must have a mutie strain in him. However, the sniper was valuable to the militia, and Zimyanin had never mentioned his suspicions to anyone.

"How many?"

"More than four hands and less than five, Major. They crossed the bottom of the trail."

"And higher?"

The sniper hesitated, pressing the Zeiss binoculars to his eyes. "Not easy against the dark rock in this light, Major."

"But?"

"But I think less than two hands. I am sorry I cannot see more."

It was enough for the major, and he took back the glasses, smiling. It had been a long stern chase, longer than he guessed when he first received his orders. Now he was in America. It lay open before him, begging to be possessed like a complaisant whore with her legs spread wide.

Tomorrow could be the best day of his life.

THE FIRST PINK FINGERS of light were creeping over the eastern side of the valley, touching the concrete of the dam. The wind had veered more to the south, bringing the promise of heavy snowfall. The air tasted foul from the volcanic sulfur carried from a volcano a few miles toward the sea.

Uchitel had wandered to the river, keeping in the lee of the huge boulders that dotted the valley. Soon it would be done, he thought. He could take the buggies of the Americans, and their new weapons. And perhaps learn from them the location of the secret city of power where such things resided.

And then there would be no stopping the Narodniki, the rulers of the land.

RYAN GLANCED AT KRYSTY who lay at his side, then turned to look up the valley toward the dam.

"Soon," said the man.

UCHITEL MOVED AWAY from his band and stood where the slope began to steepen. Four members of his band slept there, including Barkhat, Krisa and Zmeya, whose skinny frame was almost smothered by the porcine bulk of Bizabraznia. It was time to begin rousing them for the coming day.

MAJOR ZIMYANIN wiped smears of mud from the hem of his long gray coat, then peered across the valley, squinting at the unusually bright rising sun. It was rare to see it so naked and unveiled, free from chem clouds.

He clapped his hands together, trying to keep warm; it was much colder than the day before. As the officer glanced farther up the valley, he saw a pinprick of silver that trailed orange and red fringed with ragged smoke. Some moments passed before he realized what it heralded. By then the boom of the massive explosion had confirmed his guess.

Chapter Nineteen

WITHOUT THE USUAL computer-guidance system, J.B. had been forced to fire the missile on manual sighting. Fortunately the range was less than half a mile, so accuracy wasn't too much of a problem. And the target was some thousand feet long by two hundred feet high.

The explosion came nearly dead center between the middle towers, roughly a third of the way down from the top of the dam.

To J. B. Dix, standing only a little below the level of the reservoir, the effect was spectacular.

To Ryan Cawdor, halfway down the valley, it was stunningly powerful.

To Uchitel and the rest of the Narodniki, at the bottom of the valley, the sight of the explosion was totally, lethally paralyzing.

A mighty column of foaming water ripped through the hole. Immediately great cracks appeared in the main structure of the dam as the pressure began to tell. Within ten seconds a huge hole appeared, destroying the top walkway of the concrete structure. Hundreds of thousands of gallons of frothing, surging water roared into the valley, washing away everything before it.

For a few heartbeats, Ryan thought they'd miscalculated. The reservoir emptied faster than they'd figured it would, and the flood swept by only forty feet below where they hid. The noise was deafening, like the roaring of a thousand enraged animals. At his side, Krysty held her hands over her ears.

The guerrillas' camp vanished.

All but half a dozen of the Narodniki were buried under the avalanche of water, mangled and pulped by the stones that the dam burst carried with it. The corpses bobbed and danced across the plain, slowing as the water began to spread out.

The dead were borne along for a couple of miles until the water became more shallow, and the carcasses snagged on rocky outcrops. The river turned sluggish and gray at its edges, finally solidifying into ice, so the corpses rested, hands and heads sticking out from the hardening slush.

Pechal went farthest of all. Sorrow, the torturer, was on his back, legs broken, hip smashed, but miraculously still living. Only his face and one hand protruded from the ice, which set around him like stone, crushing his chest, slowing his breathing. To the last, his eyes remained open and staring.

Uchitel survived.

Bedraggled and freezing, the leader of the killers clung to a rock as the water tore at his legs. He'd climbed away from the tumbling wall of bubbling death, as had three other survivors: Bizabraznia, weeping, naked below the waist from the plucking river; Zmeya, who had climbed highest of them all, wriggling to safety like a skinned eel; and Krisa, the Rat, his red eyes wide in shock.

All the rest were gone—all the animals, provisions, guns and ammunition, swept away to destruction. Uchitel looked around, seeing that the river was already dropping fast to its original level. But the land beneath it was scoured clean.

"DAMNATION TAKE YOU! Faster, you fumbling dolts! We must get there before they can escape us."

The blowing of the dam had taken Zimyanin by surprise. Until he'd seen the silver missile sprout its fiery tail, he hadn't known then any weapon that could wreak such devastation still existed. As the smoke and spray cleared, Zimyanin made out several of his prey still alive and clinging to the sides of the valley. But he'd also seen movement on the far side, where he believed there might be more of the poverty-stricken American peasants who inhabited the region. It would be as well if he got to his countrymen first.

But so early in the morning, the cavalry were slow and clumsy in saddling and mounting. He heard moans about the cold and about the lack of food, not even a hot drink for breakfast.

But at last they were picking their way along the ridge of the valley, heading toward the final scene of the drama.

"OL' J.B. GOT THE ACE on the line," whooped Ryan Cawdor, staring unbelievingly at the chaos below him. The main torrent had abated, and the morning was so bitingly cold that the rocks on both sides of the valley were slick with ice.

"Let's go," said Finnegan, hefting his gray Heckler & Koch submachine gun.

"Watch 'em. They've probably got guns left," warned Ryan.

"Not that fat sow," grinned Henn, pointing at the huge Bizabraznia. "Unless she's got a hider pistol tucked in her snatch."

"Got room for a mortar up there," cackled Finn.

Descending with the utmost caution between the tumbled, wet stones, Ryan led them to the river. Each of them was carrying a blaster, ready for action: Hennings and Finnegan with their HK-54As, Krysty with the silvered H&K P-7A 13 pistol, Ryan with his caseless G-12, all covering the helpless Russians.

With the water now returned to its original level, Uchitel and the three other survivors climbed warily down and were now facing Ryan across fifteen paces of fast-flowing river. Slowly, Uchitel raised his hands above his head in the universal gesture of surrender.

Krisa and Zmeya followed. Finally, scowling, Biza-braznia lifted her hands.

"Watch 'em," said Ryan, crossing the jumble of stones and large boulders with care. If he slipped on the ice, the water would carry him to his death.

Once he was over, he beckoned for the others to follow. He kept his eye—and the muzzle of his blaster—pointed at the captive Russians.

"What're we goin' to do with the fuckers?" asked Finnegan.

"Ice 'em," replied Ryan. "Mebbe try an' talk to 'em first. You got that book?" he asked Uchitel and mimed reading and flicking pages.

Krysty watched a trickle of water flowing over the lip of the ruined dam. "I can see J.B., Lori and Doc near the ghost town," she said.

"They're wavin'," added Hennings.

Ryan was still watching Uchitel, his good eye locked on the Russian's amber gaze. "The book, you bastard," he repeated.

"I can hear—" began Krysty.

"What?"

"Horses. Earth Mother. I can hear so many horses, comin' this way! I couldn't hear before with the noise of the river."

"J.B. is pointin' over that way," said Hennings, gesturing to the west, where Krysty was also pointing.

Uchitel's face was impassive. He had delivered enough death in his time to know that Ryan Cawdor's face showed only the promise of killing. Moving carefully, the Russian reached inside his coat and produced the damp copy of the phrase book, throwing it down in the mud at Ryan's feet.

As he stooped to pick it up, Ryan heard what the girl had detected: hooves pounding on rock, coming toward them. He glanced toward the ghost town, but J.B., Doc and Lori had disappeared.

"Let's kill the sons of bitches and get us the fuck out of here," said Hennings, backing toward the river.

"No," said Ryan. "Look at this bastard's face. Whoever's comin' aren't friends of his. Must be Americans. We'll wait and . . ."

The words died in his throat as he watched the ridge a quarter mile to the west.

While they'd been in the redoubt, he'd seen a couple of old vids called *westerns*, involving savages that attacked villes and burned them down until sec men called *cavalry* came to the rescue. Impressively, savages always seemed to appear in single file on the crest of a hill.

"Well, I'll be . . ." whispered Finn.

Bizabraznia fell to her pale knees and buried her face in her hands. The other Russians looked scared.

"There's nearly a hundred," said Hennings with almost religious awe.

A hundred men, well mounted, all wearing a uniform, were approaching. Even at that distance, Ryan knew that these couldn't be friends or Americans. There wasn't a baron in Deathlands with the power to put a regular small army into the field like this.

The rising sun glanced off badges on some of their gray caps. Most had rifles slung across their backs.

"Any move and we're cold meat," said Ryan. "If it comes to it, take as many as you can. Play it soft."

They watched as the riders descended from the ridge, then cantered over the flat trail, reining in a wide semicircle at a signal from the man who seemed to be their leader. He was a pockmarked fellow with a bald head and a drooping moustache. He heeled his horse forward. Stopping a few paces from Ryan, he scrutinized them all, paying particular attention to their blasters.

Uchitel studied the officer, then barked a question at him in Russian. Zimyanin ignored him.

Ryan tried to flick through the phrase book while still keeping his gun ready. The bald man reached into his coat, pulling out a small red notebook, with some writing on the cover in a peculiar, angular script that Ryan couldn't read.

"I am Major Gregori Zimyanin, and I bring greetings from the party."

The accent was heavy, but Ryan found it easier to understand than Uchitel's garbled words. He bowed slightly to the Russian.

"I take prisoner this mans," he said, waving with the book at Uchitel and the other three.

"Let him," hissed Finnegan.

"No," said Ryan. "They're my prisoners."

Zimyanin glanced through his book as if he wasn't sure he believed what he said. "*Nyet*. I take. He Russian. I take."

"No," repeated Ryan, conscious of the others spreading out behind him supportively.

The officer pored over his book, lips moving as he rehearsed what he wanted to say. "You are four. We are many. We kill."

"We kill many of you," answered Ryan, trying to show a confidence he didn't truly feel.

"He Russian," the major said, pointing at Uchitel again.

Ryan made his move. Taking care not to spark off a firefight, he stepped in and moved Uchitel and the woman to one side with the barrel of the Heckler & Koch. Then he pushed the other two prisoners toward the man on horseback.

"I'm a great believer in compromise," he said, knowing that the soldier would not understand; knowing as well that the gesture was obvious.

Zimyanin hesitated. He could see that these Americans were not helpless peasants. They could only be some sort of unofficial militia, roaming the land to repel invaders. There weren't many of them, but their guns looked more lethal than anything he'd ever seen before. And they'd blown that huge dam.

Ryan faced him, raising his eye questioningly. "Yes, my friend?"

"Da."

The smooth, gray rifle slipped inside the long coat. Ryan drew the SIG-Sauer P-226 9 mm pistol, relishing the familiar weight in his hand. Standing three paces from Uchitel and the blubbery bulk of the woman, he fired three spaced shots.

The first two entered the woman's chest between her sagging breasts. The impact sent Bizabraznia staggering backward, and Ryan put the third bullet carefully into the middle of her face.

The entrance hole of the final shot was lost in the pasty expanse of her round face with its layers of jowls. It hit the center of the upper lip and exited near the top of her head, removing a chunk of skull as large as a grown man's fist.

Instantly there was some talk among the watching horsemen, but Ryan couldn't tell whether it was from approval or anger. He stepped toward Uchitel, who faced him impassively.

"Nyet," Zimyanin called then rattled off a string of commands in Russian. He pointed toward Zmeya and Krisa, who fell to their knees and began to babble their pleas for mercy.

The Americans watched as six soldiers swung down from their horses. One man took Zmeya's left hand in both of his while a second cavalryman took the other hand. They tugged as hard as they could to get the kneeling guerrilla to rise. While they pulled him, a third soldier took a short length of waxed rawhide from his belt and looped it around Zmeya's neck.

The other trio of cavalrymen treated Krisa to the same, then looked toward the commanding officer for a signal. Zimyanin favored Ryan with a thin smile, then nodded to the troops.

The nooses of thin cord tightened, vanishing into the necks of both condemned men. Zmeya tried to cry out, but the sound was strangled, caught in his throat. The soldiers holding the prisoners struggled to retain a footing on the slippery pebbles. Krisa died first, his red eyes protruding so far from their sockets that it seemed they would burst. Blood came from his mouth and nose, then from the corners of his eyes. His body went suddenly slack.

Zmeya, the Snake, fought harder, and his passing took longer. Blood was jetting from a severed artery under his ear before he finally became limp, slumping in the arms of the two men gripping his wrists.

At a gesture from Zimyanin, the corpses were dragged by the ankles to the river. One of the soldiers drew a steel knife from his belt and sliced the ears off both bodies and tucked the ears into a pocket.

Then each carcass was heaved into the river. Rolling and turning in the swift current, they were carried away across the plain, toward where the rest of Uchitel's band had found their last resting place.

"My turn, Major," said Ryan, ready to execute Uchitel. But the chief of the butchers was not quite done yet.

With a curse he pushed Ryan into Hennings and Finnegan, then produced a battered 9 mm Makarov PM pistol from inside his coat and levelled it at Zimyanin. Time held still, like a bubble of air in a frozen lake. The officer's face whitened, his hands rising in a futile gesture of protection.

The crack of the handgun was almost swallowed by the rushing noise of the river.

Uchitel's almond-shaped golden eyes opened wide in disbelief, and he looked over his shoulder at the flame-haired Krysty Wroth and at the small gleaming H & K pistol smoking in her right hand. Blood appeared on his chest as he dropped his own gun in the dirt, sank to his knees, then toppled, his silver headband with its great ruby clinking against the stones.

"Earth Mother forgive me," whispered the girl.

"She will, lover. She will," said Ryan.

The Americans did nothing to stop the soldiers from mutilating the corpses of the woman and Uchitel, though Hennings pushed them aside to retrieve the fallen piece of jewelry.

"Take it, girl," urged the tall black, handing the ruby to Krysty. "Better you than them. You fuckin' earned it."

The two corpses bobbed downriver, ending the short and bloody history of the Narodniki.

Zimyanin had been diligently studying his phrase book again. Ryan had thumbed through the brown paperback that had belonged to Uchitel. The Russian spoke first.

"I thank you for your assistance. Now we take all your country for party."

"What? No fuckin' way, friend."

Ryan's gesture and tone needed no translation. The officer indicated his overwhelmingly superior forces with a wave of his hand. "Your country is not strong. We take. You not veto us."

It was the moment that Ryan Cawdor had suspected was coming from the time the Russians first appeared over the ridge. They must have ridden across many miles of Alaska and seen no opposition. Now only three men and a girl seemed to stand between them and all of America.

"Let 'em go. We can make the redoubt and get the fuck out of here."

Finn's argument was unanswerable. To fight here was to die. If they stood aside, it was better than fifty-fifty that the Russians wouldn't provoke a firefight, and the gateway would carry them far from here. This bitter northern land with its freezing residue of the nuclear winter wasn't their concern. There surely wasn't any profit in trying to defend it.

Ryan hesitated only a moment.

"No," he said.

"Nyet?" asked Zimyanin in disbelief.

"No. This is our land. You get back to Russia and your party. Go."

"You fight?"

"Damned right we do." He drew the G-12 again, emphasizing his point.

The Russian thumbed through his book frantically. Eventually he seemed to find what he wanted. "You will die all. Why?"

"Friend of mine back in Deathlands once took off all his gear and jumped in a tar pit. I got him out, cleaned him down and asked him the same question—asked him why. He said it seemed a fuckin' good idea at the time."

Zimyanin looked at Ryan, finding him utterly beyond comprehension. Behind Ryan, Henn and Finnegan laughed at his story.

"Ready," said Ryan. "Here it comes."

There was a sudden burst of automatic-weapons fire, faint and distant, high up the valley, toward the ghost town. Everyone looked around, seeing three figures grouped around something: a pointed object about as tall as a man.

"It's the fuckin' dummy missile," gasped Hennings.

"Shut up," snarled Ryan.

Zimyanin took his precious Zeiss binoculars from their leather case and raised them to his eyes, adjusting the focus. He held them there for a long time, finally lowering them.

Silently, ignoring the whispers from his troops, he swung off his horse and stood holding the reins. The book open in his gloved right hand, the Russian beckoned to Ryan, then gestured at the missile.

But he couldn't find what he wanted to ask. Shaking his head, clicking his fingers in irritation, finally sighing, he pointed again toward J.B. and the rocket.

"Boom?" he asked, hesitantly.

"Yeah. Boom! Fuckin' great boom! *Boooooom!*"

"Da," agreed the Russian, searching assiduously again for the phrase he wanted. Eventually he found it.

"To your good health, American, and to your land."

He offered a hand, and Ryan reached out and took it, shaking it firmly. He looked into the eyes of the Russian.

"And to your good health, brother, and to your country and party."

Zimyanin clicked his heels and bowed slightly. Remounting he called out an order to his patrol, then led them slowly across the valley toward the west.

Toward the icebound Bering Strait.

Toward Russia.

About a half-mile away he stood in the stirrups, and raised a clenched fist to the watching Americans. Ryan waved in acknowledgement.

Finally the last of the cavalry unit vanished over the ridge and the day was quiet again.

"That was close, lover," said Krysty, finally holstering her pistol.

"Yeah," agreed Ryan. "It was close."

Epilogue

THE CODE FOR THE OUTER DOOR of the redoubt, 108J, worked, and they trooped inside, leaving the two buggies out on the plateau for the local muties to find. Inside the cavernous building, the temperature had fallen since the time they left only a couple of days earlier. Many of the lights were either flickering or extinguished.

They spent an hour stocking up on food and ammunition, then using J.B.'s map, made their way to the gateway on the fourth level.

"Goin' to try a code, Doc?" asked J.B.

"I fear there would be little point. I think we must trust to the random element and hope we finish somewhere better than this wasteland."

"Somewhere warmer, Doc, if you don't mind," Henn put in, grinning.

Ryan was last into the chamber, with its now-familiar floor and ceiling patterns, and its strange glasslike walls. Everyone sat down, with Krysty pulling at Lori's arm to show her what to do. The girl had shown signs of great nervousness as they moved through the redoubt where she'd spent all her life, but her trust in the others carried her along. Now she sat with them on the floor.

"It's like a quick sleep and then a bad headache," said Finnegan to her. "We wake somewhere else."

"Somewhere good?" she asked.

"Who knows?" answered Ryan. "Everyone ready? Then here we go."

He closed the door firmly. The lights began to gleam and dance. He had just enough time to sit down before he felt the jump beginning.

THE INSIDE OF HIS BRAIN felt as if it had been chopped into a million splinters, then flushed down a dark, echoing drain.

Ryan Cawdor blinked open his eye and looked around. The first thing he noticed was that the chamber was uncomfortably hot.

ERIC HELM

VIETNAM: GROUND ZERO

An elite jungle fighting group of strike-and-hide specialists fight a dirty war half a world away from home. This is more than action adventure. Every novel in this series is a piece of Vietnam history brought to life, from the Battle for Hill 875 to the Tet Offensive and the terror of the infamous Hanoi Hilton POW camp, told through the eyes of an American Special Forces squad. These books cut close to the bone, telling it the way it really was.

"Vietnam at Ground Zero is where this book is written. The author has been there, and he knows. I salute him and I recommend this book to my friends."

—Don Pendleton,
creator of The Executioner

Now available from Gold Eagle Books, #1 publisher of adventures.

Mack Bolan's

by Dick Stivers

Action writhes in the reader's own streets
as Able Team's Carl "Ironman" Lyons,
Pol Blancanales and Gadgets Schwarz
make triple trouble in blazing war. Join
Dick Stivers's Able Team as it returns to
the United States to become the country's
finest tactical neutralization squad in an
era of urban terror and unbridled crime.

"Able Team will go anywhere, do anything,
in order to complete their mission. Plenty
of action! Recommended!"
—*West Coast Review of Books*

Able Team titles are available
wherever paperbacks are sold.

GOLD
EAGLE

AT-1

Mack Bolan's

PHOENIX FORCE

by Gar Wilson

The battle-hardened, five-man commando unit known as Phoenix Force continues its onslaught against the hard realities of global terrorism in an endless crusade for freedom, justice and the rights of the individual. Schooled in guerrilla warfare, equipped with the latest in lethal weapons, Phoenix Force's adventures have made them a legend in their own time. Phoenix Force is the free world's foreign legion!

"Gar Wilson is excellent! Raw action attacks the reader on every page."

—Don Pendleton

GOLD EAGLE

Phoenix Force titles are available wherever paperbacks are sold.

PF-1

**Nile Barrabas and the
Soldiers of Barrabas are the**

SOBs

by Jack Hild

Nile Barrabas is a nervy son of a bitch who
was the last American soldier out of Vietnam
and the first man into a new kind of action. His
warriors, called the Soldiers of Barrabas, have
one very simple ambition: to do what the
Marines can't or won't do. Join the Barrabas
blitz! Each book hits new heights—this is
brawling at its best!

"Nile Barrabas is one tough SOB himself. . . .
A wealth of detail. . . . SOBs does the job!"
                        —*West Coast Review of Books*